The Case of the Invisible Souls

A Jarvis Mann Detective Novella

By
R Weir

Copyediting by:
YM Zachery and JB Joseph Editing Services

Cover Design by:
Happi Anarky
www.happianarky.com

Cover Concept by:
Dakota Weir

To those Invisible Souls
on the street corner,
may you find your way

Thanks to all of my beta readers,
who helped make
The Case of the Invisible Souls
the best it could be.

Chapter 1

December winter in Denver can be bone-chilling cold. But the blustery winds take it to a bitter extreme. I ran despite all of this, jogging to build endurance, the frost clinging for dear life to my cheeks and exposed skin. The temperature showed twenty-seven degrees when I left early this morning, but it felt much chillier as I cruised up the back alley from Warren Avenue on the tail end of my run. Snow remained on the ground around me, from a five-inch storm two days earlier, and I maneuvered around the slick spots where the sun had melted and re-froze the moisture overnight.

When I reached my parking lot, I slowed down to walk the final distance, my heart racing, breath billowing in visible puffs through the air. I wore spandex from top to bottom, with sweatpants and a sweatshirt sporting a Colorado flag emblem providing a top layer.

Thin gloves were worn to keep my fingers from freezing completely, yet I was warm from the sweating underneath, though frosty where the wind struck me.

I reached for my keys when I noticed a man combing through the large, metal, deep-green trash dumpster, searching for who knows what. There was a Safeway shopping cart, filled with all the person's possessions close at hand. Much of it packed in black leaf bags to protect it from the cruel winter weather. He was determined to find what he was looking for, but wasn't making a mess in his quest, so I let him be.

I strolled down my steps, avoiding the slick spots. Once inside I felt the heat immediately, thankful for the gas-flamed warmth of my furnace and to be out of the wind, with a roof over my head to keep me dry and secure.

Stripping off my gloves and sweatshirt, I reached for some cold bottled water in my fridge. It seemed odd I'd want cold liquid on this frosty day, but it tasted good going down, quenching a thirst brought on by the jogging. Finding a brick of cheddar cheese, I sliced off a few chunks to fill the caloric need that rumbled through my stomach. I checked my phone for messages but there weren't any.

Putting the phone down, I turned and was about to go and enjoy a hot shower when there was a knock on my door. Looking out the

1

window, I saw the same man who had been rummaging through the trash. I hesitated to answer—for whatever reason I was uncertain why.

"May I help you?" I asked, the door only partially open, mostly to keep the chill out of my space, or so I told myself.

"Sorry to bother you," replied the man, with a beard and stocking cap to protect his head and face from the winter air. "I saw your sign outside. Are you Jarvis Mann, the private detective?"

Again, I hesitated. *Silly of me.* For an unknown reason I seemed nervous about dealing with him. I had faced gangsters and shady characters many times in my line of work, but for some reason a homeless man gave me pause.

"I am," I finally answered. "Are you in need of assistance?"

"Yes. Several companions of mine are missing and I wondered if you might be able to help me find them."

The gentleman looked familiar. I wasn't sure what it was, but I seemed to remember him from somewhere. I weighed the odds and figured he couldn't harm me any more than the next person, so I opened the door completely to let him in.

"Come in and have a seat," I declared, while pointing to my kitchen table and chairs.

He removed his stocking cap and ran his gloved hands through his long hair, before unzipping his heavy worn chocolate colored coat. Taking a seat, you could hear his black ski pant crunching when they touched the chair. His clothes were older, showing a bit of wear, but in good shape overall, including heavy boots. He didn't smell bad—maybe a day or two removed from bathing. I wondered where he lived and spent his days and nights. I was cold after jogging for forty-five minutes. I couldn't imagine living in the clutches of an unforgiving winter every second of the day.

"Thank you," he announced happily. "Most wouldn't have let me in."

I didn't comment on the fact that I almost didn't, instead offering him a reassuring smile.

"No problem. Can I get you a liquid refreshment?"

"If you have some cold water that would be great."

I grabbed him a plastic bottle from the fridge and placed it before him. Apparently, he didn't think it was odd drinking a chilled liquid on a cold day either.

"What can I help you with?" I probed. "You mentioned some friends of yours are missing."

He stopped to choose his words, eyes scanning downward as if he was nervous, while trying to get comfortable in my chair. I had to admit the hardwood didn't conform well to my rear end either and it might be time to upgrade.

"There are some of us in the homeless community that gather together on Broadway, near an old abandoned building," he stated, his eyes now looking at me. "It is mostly a living space we cohabitate in. Some residing there are more sociable than others, but we're mostly neighborly and get along, even at times helping each other."

He stopped to twist off the top and take a drink of his water before continuing, letting out a pleasing sigh at the refreshment. "We've had a few...*visitors* recently. Most of them aren't sociable. Stop by to harass us and call us bums. Some young punks with nothing to do. We try to ignore them, but it's not easy when they come around and mess with our possessions. Dumping over our shopping carts, stepping on and tearing apart our makeshift shelters. It's bad enough we're out on the streets trying to survive without dealing with losers like that."

What he told me was aggravating to hear. Why people with so much, would often demean those with so little, baffled me. It made my heart sick at their cruelty. I wondered if he was searching for a bodyguard. *Enforcer for the homeless.* More employment data to add to my resume.

"Have you ever flagged down a cop and get them involved?" I inquired.

He grimaced at my words. "No. They don't have time for us. Think we're all drunks or crazy insane. Don't get me wrong some of us are. Been dumped out on the streets when the Federal money ran dry. A lot of hurting former soldiers in the lot, that the VA can't take in or care for anymore."

I had certainly formed a similar opinion through the years about homeless people. It was too easy to fault the person for his troubles, when many other factors contributed. His words shed a great deal of light, opening my eyes to other possibilities.

At that point, I remembered where I knew him from. He often

sat on the corner of Broadway and Evans with a sign saying he was a veteran and homeless, asking for spare change to buy food. I had handed him a few bills through the years, when I had extras burning a hole in my wallet.

"I've seen you," I proclaimed. "Handed you money a few times in the past."

He nodded with a half-smile. "I remember. Once you had a business card wrapped in the bills you gave me, probably by mistake. I held onto it. When you don't have much, you keep everything. I dug through my stuff and found it, thinking I could locate you and ask for help."

"Are you really a veteran?" Not sure why I questioned if he was, for there was no reason to lie.

"Yes. I fought in the first Iraq war. I was wounded, but still went back to complete my tour afterwards. I had mental issues that required help and made it hard to work when I got home. I received assistance for a while, but that ended and here I am."

I shook my head in spite for his situation, his words heartbreaking to hear. I had the utmost respect for those who protect our country and the pain many of them go through during and after the battle.

"Sorry. Not the American dream you hoped for."

If there was sadness or bitterness, he didn't display it. It had been going on for so long, maybe he was numb to his situation.

"No, it's more of a nightmare than a dream," he stated with no emotion. "There are others out there like me. I did my duty for my country, but my country failed me, as it failed the others. It's challenging, but I'm surviving."

It was a shame to hear and see. The motto *"We don't leave our people behind"* didn't always apply once the fighting was over, even though the war still wages on in their being.

"You mentioned people bothering you, but not about your companions disappearing."

He stopped to take another drink of water, savoring it, as if it were a fine wine before continuing.

"One day two men showed up in a fancy black SUV while the punks were screwing with us and ran them off, telling them in a convincing and aggressive manner to never come around again. They pushed them around pretty good. Scared the hell out of them.

4

It was like a godsend as we were sick of the harassment but not strong enough to fight them off."

My face contorted at his words. "A miracle?"

"Yes. They were all polite and apologetic. Seemingly feeling sorry for us. After several minutes of chit-chat, they mention they're looking for a couple of strong men for jobs. Will pay them cash if they get in the SUV and come with them. I'm a little leery and have trust issues, so I said no thanks." His eyes scanned downward, embarrassed at this shortcoming. "But a couple of the men are desperate and hadn't had much to eat for a week or so. Their handouts had been trailing off. They go with them, leaving everything they own in the world behind and we never see them again."

"Seems a long shot, they'd be given jobs and no longer needed to be on the street?" I proclaimed, uncertain what this meant.

"Exactly. That would be one miracle I can't imagine happening."

"Sounds like there were others."

"Yes. The same men came back a few days later, claiming the two were working out great and had employment for more. There was some resistance this time, but they gave them crisp new one hundred-dollar bills as a lure. That kind of money is hard to resist. Three more were gone, never to be seen again. It's happened three more times, this last time to my closest friend who couldn't turn down their offer. The two men were experts at selling it, saying everyone they had taken before were now working, happy in their new lives and had been provided a place to live. I told him not to do it and asked for some verifiable proof, but he went anyway. That was a week ago and there has been no sign of him. There is no possibility he wouldn't have tried to find a way to contact me. Something fishy is going on."

"Any rumblings from other homeless in the area?" I inquired.

"I get around and talk, learning others are being approached— so yes. We're always moving to keep from being bored and frozen. It isn't hard to find us. We're often standing on street corners, carrying signs. A few will ignore you, while others like to chat."

All of this seemed extremely odd and difficult for me to believe. Luring people away to do what? And to go where? Could it all have been in his mind? He said he had mental health issues after coming back from the war. Was it possible it was all in his head?

"Is there anyone that can confirm your story?" I asked.

"You can come down to our habitat and ask around?"

For some reason, I didn't trust his word, at least completely. And I wasn't sure I could trust others within his group of homeless people.

"Anyone else? Maybe someone not part of your community."

He glared at me, a bit perturbed I was questioning him. He thought for a minute before answering.

"Pastor Sam at the Mission we go to, just off Broadway, a few blocks south of here."

I leaned back in the uncomfortable chair, arms crossed, thinking about it for a few minutes. I had no pressing cases, or as a matter of fact, any cases right now. If what he said was true, then I was curious about what was going on. At the very least I could lend a pro-bono hand in solving the mystery.

"What is the name of the place where Pastor Sam works?"

"The Mission of the Invisible Souls."

Chapter 2

Before he left, I got his name. Parker Turner made it clear he couldn't pay me, but I told him not to worry. I would spend a couple of days investigating to see what I found. At least it would keep me from being bored during this slow time, and I'd already completed my Christmas shopping.

I offered him a sandwich, chips and another bottle of water, which he accepted, stuffing them in a backpack he was carrying. Shaking my hand, he thanked me, before going on his way out into the blustery cold. He told me the best place to find him, and I promised I'd provide an update in a day or so.

After showering, I changed clothes and hopped into my classic 69' Mustang. I'd never been to The Mission of the Invisible Souls before, and with the help of my phone, I located it, arriving there in short order, curious at what I'd find.

I had called ahead and when I walked in was met by an older, silver haired lady, Louise. She was gracious, spunky and full of life as she gave me a tour of the place, which was down Broadway and a block west. She explained that the building was an old apartment complex that had been abandoned and condemned. It had been falling apart, in an area where many of the buildings were pre-World War II. The owners could no longer afford the upkeep, so the city shut them down and seized the structure to cover back taxes due. A church west of them bought it eight years ago for next to nothing from the City of Denver.

As part of the agreement, they slowly fixed it up, using donations of money, materials and labor over a couple of years, gradually making it livable for those on the streets to come and find a place to live or spend a night out of the cold. All that was left of the building was the outside red brick shell. Inside was totally redesigned for their needs. The rooms provided small living areas, beds to sleep in, bathrooms with showers, and in some cases, a basic kitchen.

The nicer places for the more permanent residents and those with children were on the upper of the three floors, with multiple sleeping quarters and a private bathroom. The second-floor rooms had a smaller living space, a single bedroom, with communal bathrooms. The first-floor had a modern kitchen and a large shared dining area using a third of the floor, while the rest was mostly open space for cots when they were overflowing, especially during the cold winter months.

The whole place was kept clean and in excellent shape for the throngs of people that wandered through. There were strict rules to be followed by everyone. No booze, no drugs, no fighting, no weapons and no sexual liaisons. Everyone had to pull their own weight and pitch in if they were to stay for any length of time; whether it be cleaning, food prep or simple maintenance. Louise explained every detail proudly. As people passed, she would say hello, knowing the first names of everyone we saw. It was an impressive operation, doing extraordinary work, during difficult times.

As the tour came to an end, Louise led me to the main office of Pastor Sam. Being the chauvinist I was, I'd assumed Sam was a man. But it was Samantha, an African American woman, nearly my size in height, though not as heavy, but still with some arm and shoulder muscles to go with her military tattoos. One with the flag and bald eagle, saying *"Freedom isn't Free"* adorned her left bicep. Her hair was straight, long, just over the shoulders and dyed a lavender color with blonde highlights and held back with a stars and stripes bandana. Faded blue-jeans covered her legs, a sleeveless black top tightly gripping her fit upper body. She must have liked the cool air, as it was chilly, even in her office.

She welcomed me with a firm handshake and offered up a chair in her sparse workspace. I handed over my business card, which she read before taking a seat behind her wooden desk.

"Wow, a real-life gumshoe," she announced with a deep voice and joyous smile. "Hopefully you aren't carrying. We don't allow guns inside our facility."

I opened my brown leather jacket, so she could see I wasn't armed.

"I don't like to carry unless absolutely necessary. It ruins the body line of my coat," I declared with a grin.

"What can I help you with, Mister Mann?" she said while smiling at my humor, her hands linked together sitting in her lap.

"Please call me Jarvis. This is quite an impressive facility you have here."

"It was a rat-infested hellhole at first," Sam uttered with distain. "Lots of sweat equity to make it livable."

"How long has it been open for?"

"Parts of it for short of seven years. It took twenty-two months to bring it up to code to be fully operational."

I nodded, impressed by the achievement.

"You've been running things since day one?" I inquired.

She stopped and grabbed an empty white coffee cup and went over to her drip machine to fill up. On the cup in black lettering read *"Human Rights are not Optional."* A sentiment I shared.

"Would you like some?" she asked. "I have to warn you, I make it strong."

I made a sour face. "No thanks. I try to avoid caffeine whenever possible."

"I wish I could. In all my years it's the one vice I haven't been able to shake."

She sat back down after taking a long pleasurable sip, holding the warm cup in both hands. I noticed a few plaques on the walls, given for service to her country. On top of a filing cabinet were some pictures of her and family, and her posing with fellow soldiers.

"To answer your question, I've only been running this place for three years now. When it first opened, I was a member trying to find my way. I too lived on the streets. If it weren't for the Mission, I'm not sure where I'd be now."

"Not an easy life to live on the streets," I declared. "Even more challenging for a woman on her own."

"It was. I made a few acquaintances out there. Found a couple I could trust. But was always cautious of those who might take advantage."

"From your tattoo and pictures in your office, I guess you were in the military?"

"In the Army. I did a tour in Iraq and some time in Afghanistan." The gleam in her eye showed the pride in her service.

"A tough adjustment period when you returned?" I wondered.

She nodded her head. "Have you been to war—in combat, Jarvis?"

I shook my head. "Not like a soldier in a war zone like you

9

have. But I've been in my fair share of battles where people I've known have been killed."

"Does it haunt you?" She studied me with genuine interest in my answer.

"At times, yes."

She took in the fresh aroma from her coffee cup, seemingly soothing her, as she closed her eyes. It took her a minute to respond, her open gaze now staring in the distance.

"It haunted me for many a day. Consuming me so I couldn't work or relate to other people. In time, I was able to get past it. It still haunts me, but I'm at ease with feeling bad about all the crazy shit which happened over there. It no longer paralyzes me. I'm a functioning human being again. I try to help others who were in the same boat. Those are rocky waters many need guidance to navigate through."

"Is one of those Parker Turner?" I inquired, curious if she knew him.

"Yes," she replied knowingly, familiar with the name. "He is one of those that stays here from time to time. Has he done something wrong?"

"No. He came to me for assistance. Said you could verify something going on in the homeless community around here."

This seemed to pique her interest, as she leaned forward in her chair, arms resting on the tabletop, coffee cup still in hand. "Concerning?"

"Friends of his who've gone missing. Taken away by two men, offering money and employment, never to return."

She took another long savoring sip on her java, her eyes closed, thinking how to answer.

"There have been rumblings," she noted, her eyes now open, gazing at me. "And I've noticed smaller crowds coming in these last few weeks. Which is surprising since it's been so cold. On these brutal winter nights, we are normally overflowing with people needing shelter."

My interest was piqued now. "What rumblings have you heard?"

"Much as what Parker told you. Men waving around cash and promising jobs. Anyone going with them not returning. Sometimes they were more forceful and intimidating to get them to cooperate.

10

We had a visit the other day. Two men flashing around money and making bold promises. I told them in no uncertain terms to leave."

"Have you reported this to authorities?"

Her neatly trimmed eyebrows raised in irritation. "Jarvis, I have my hands full keeping this place running. Other than the church and our sponsors, we get little help from the powers that be. They truly wish we were invisible and disappear into the night. We call them, but we aren't a priority."

I understood them being skeptical. So was I when hearing what Parker claimed. Yet somewhere in the back of my head, was a nagging suspicion something nefarious was going on. And when it came to mysteries, I liked to approach them head-on and find answers where no one else can.

"I have some free time, so I may snoop around—see what I can find. Any reason you can think of why I shouldn't?"

"Nothing comes to mind. If I can lend any assistance let me know. Though, from your physique, there's little doubt you're capable of handling yourself."

I smiled, to let her know, yes I could, resisting the urge to flex my biceps, when I heard some commotion. Louise came running in faster than I imagined someone her age could move. She was startled and looked panicky.

"Those two men are back!" she said out of breath.

"The ones from a couple of days ago?" asked Sam with concern in her tone.

"Yes. And they're bothering people again."

"Call the police, Louise, and wait here."

Sam got out of her chair swiftly after sitting down her coffee cup and moved with authority. She too appeared to be someone who could handle herself, but I followed to lend assistance if necessary.

As we arrived at the main dining area, two men were going around, being pushy, flashing money at the patrons who were only trying to eat the meal provided, doing their best to ignore them. Both were decent size—lean, muscular, and Caucasian. One with short close-cropped hair, the other's head was shaved clean. Each had jeans, snow boots and heavy hooded coats, unzipped with sweat shirts underneath.

As Sam entered the room, she shouted out to them to halt what they were doing. Both turned around, glared at her and started smiling.

"Look at the lovely black lady acting tough," announced the first one with the shaved head.

"We're here just trying to help people," added the other, money in his hands. "Offering them cash to work."

"I doubt that," replied Sam. "As I told you the other day, you aren't welcome here."

"Might even have a job for *you*," claimed the one with the shaved head. "Be my date for the night and get paid well."

He grinned ear to ear, as if he was god's gift to women. Their boasts of why they were there adding credence to what Parker had claimed. I wanted to step over and knock some sense into his bald head, but Sam walked over to face him with a stare of confidence and no fear on her perturbed face.

"Leave now before the police show, or I will *make* you leave," she said coolly.

"You think you can," he said, while trying to grab her chest.

As his hand came forward, Sam grabbed his wrist, twisted his arm behind his back and slammed him to the table top with a loud thud, pinning him down so he couldn't move. You could hear the air go out of his body as he gasped to fill his lungs with needed oxygen. His friend made a move and she sensed it, kicking him square in the testicles with her pointed boots, all the while still holding down the bald one. He clutched at his groin, dropping to his knees, feeling a pain no man enjoys.

I watched with pleasure, noticing my hands were fists, ready to strike. But I relaxed my fingers as she clearly had the situation under control. The way she had forcefully handled the two men was hard not to admire.

"Now I'm going to let you boys walk on out of here before the police arrive," she proclaimed firmly and calmly. "But if you ever come back, I won't be so forgiving. These poor people have it bad enough without idiots like you manipulating them for your own gain. Now go on and try to accomplish something honorable for once in your miserable lives."

Sam released the bald man and stepped back. He stood clutching his arm, rubbing at his elbow and shoulder. He was mad, glancing around a bit embarrassed, but too fearful to try anything else. He pulled up his partner and they headed for the exit, never once looking back.

Chasing after them, I went to make sure they didn't do anything stupid outside. They jumped into a big black Ford Expedition and drove away, as I took snapshots of them, the SUV and their license plates with my phone. All of which I shared with the police, who finally arrived twenty minutes later, showing the Mission and their patrons weren't a priority.

Chapter 3

I sent the police the pictures and gave them my statement, as did Sam. They said they'd investigate, but I didn't hold out much hope of any resolution from the sound of apathy in their tone. As Sam had said, they weren't a priority compared to everything else the police had to deal with. For now, it would appear it was up to me to get to the bottom of what was going on.

Sam shared some additional information, about how someone was trying to force the shelter out of the neighborhood. The church had been offered money to sell the building, though she wasn't sure by whom. But there had been a significant amount of real estate activity in the area, with someone buying up a lot of the old rundown buildings on either side of Broadway. What they wanted them for was unknown. But the church had held its ground, knowing there was a strong need in the area to provide for the homeless. They weren't in this to make a profit, only to help those less fortunate. But now that homeless people appeared to be disappearing, the need was waning. It could be a coincidence, but that seemed unlikely. More to the mystery, that I planned to unravel.

Since I had a plate number, I used my contacts with Denver PD and found out it was owned by a local construction company, Boss Builders Co. Assuming they weren't owned by Bruce Springsteen, I went on the web to do some research. They were a small, local construction company that had been bought up recently by a capital company named Liquid Investors.

They were a large investment company buying up businesses all around the country, many of which were in bad shape and bought out in friendly or hostile takeovers. Much of the information though wasn't available on the web, as deals like this were often confidential in nature. I needed to find a source that might know more about them. I decided to turn to my one business and construction contact, Brandon Sparks.

The owner of Sparks Builders Inc. had provided me information and support in the past. His money and influence were powerful in the Mile-High City. But his stature had likely come from not only his construction business, but from a background in the crime world. He never admitted as much to me, but it seemed likely from the power he wielded and the dangerous contacts he'd built through the years. Nevertheless, he was a reliable resource to have, and he agreed to meet me for lunch on the west side of town at one of his favorite restaurants, 240 Union.

When I arrived, it was late for lunch, but still early for dinner. But that didn't matter as I was hungry. Brandon was seated at a table for four, set with pure white table cloth, crystal wine glasses, and sparkling silverware wrapped in ebony cloth napkins. He was dipping shrimp into some cocktail sauce, his expression of glee showing his enjoyment of the seafood.

He was taller and older than I was, which I imagined to be middle fifties, hardly looking his age, other than the specks of gray in his hair. He was dressed a little more causal today; buttoned down white shirt, and black jeans, though neatly pressed and expensive. He stood and put out his hand, clamping my own as we shook. There was a local beer waiting for me, one of my favorites, while he sipped a Jack Daniels, his nectar of life. I'd never seen him drink anything else other than water. He waved for me to sit and have some shrimp which I did, though I found the sauce to be a bit on the fiery side.

"Jarvis, you're looking well," he noted after putting down his now empty glass. "It has been some time since we've talked."

The waiter was on high alert and had another JD within reach in a matter of seconds. Brandon thanked him and took another sip. I often thought his blood, if tested, would come back as half whiskey.

"Yes, back in Iowa.," I said. "Couldn't thank you enough for the help you gave me."

"Happy to provide helpful assistance. It turned out fruitful for me, as I now have aligned myself with Max Groves, and we have done some business together. That would have never happened when the 'The Bull' was in charge."

The names were two of those powerful contacts, ones that led me to believe in his unlawful ties, for Max had taken over The Bull's criminal empire.

"I'm glad it worked out for you in the end. For me it brought closure to the whole mess my brother had gotten into."

"How is your sister-in-law and niece doing?"

15

"So far so good. Helen and Jolene have gotten on with their lives. I believe Helen was even seeing someone last time I'd talked to her."

The waiter returned asking what we desired. Brandon ordered the Canadian salmon, while I decided on the pork loin. I swallowed down some ice water trying to cool my palate from the cocktail sauce, only slightly worried the alcohol in the beer would ignite in my mouth.

"We can reminisce all we want about our great times together," remarked Brandon. "But I'm sure you didn't drive out here only to wax poetic about our past adventures."

Straight and to the point was fine with me, as I took a drink of my beer, the fire in my mouth temporarily soothed. Time to get down to business.

"Have you heard of a construction company, Boss Builders?" I queried.

"Vaguely," he remarked with a wave of his hands, as if they were of no consequence. "Seems as if they're a small outfit from what I recall. I know all the big players across the country who build here in Denver, but the little ones I often don't concern myself with. Why are you asking?"

"Two men working for them came and caused a disturbance at a homeless shelter I was visiting relating to a case I'm working on. I was wondering if you'd crossed paths with them before."

"Nothing comes to mind in relation to them."

"They were recently bought out by a company called Liquid Investors. Have you heard of them?"

Brandon immediately reacted to the name, a stern expression on his mug, as he finished the last of the shrimp. He carefully pulled the napkin from his lap and patted his lips, before another drink of his JD.

"I know of Liquid Investors. They're a capital investing group, looking to buy up bargains where they can find them, strip them of what they're worth and then spit them out if there is nothing left of value." The last several words he stated with distain.

"What type of bargains are they looking for?"

"Anything they think will work for them. They buy all types of businesses, normally those in trouble, real estate that's undervalued or in foreclosure. They've been known to manipulate the worth

16

however they can, to get them the best possible price. They're sharks in the water searching for blood. If they can't find it, they will cut, claw and sever, so they can exploit the market, until it suits their needs."

It sounded as if this might be a clue. If they wanted the property the Mission was occupying, they could be trying to force them out by whatever means necessary. The question was—what this had to do with the missing homeless?

"From what I could find on the internet, Liquid Investors seems to be a faceless company," I declared. "I couldn't find anything on who was running it or calling the shots."

"There are numerous layers, as is the case for many of these capital firms. But I know of the one man who hides behind the scenes calling most of the shots. Have you heard of Powers USA Inc?"

I shook my head, for it was an unfamiliar name.

"It is run by Tyrell Powers. He is a ruthless business man on the east coast. Doesn't like competition and will do what it takes to eliminate them. And he has begun to expand into Colorado, trying to take competitors out in his path."

"Including you?" I wondered, knowing Brandon would be a formidable foe.

"He is trying, but I'm no powderpuff executive," he declared, with more distain. "But that isn't stopping him. For now, he is taking over the small fish, building his local empire, so he can challenge me. From those I've talked with, he'll be one of the toughest adversaries I will ever face."

"Certainly trampling on homeless isn't out of the realm of possibilities," I proclaimed after finishing my beer.

"I wouldn't put it past him and his organization. If it gets in the way of their grand plan, it would be of no consequence."

Our meals arrived, a fresh beer replacing the empty one as I dug in. Hearing the horrors of the world hadn't ruined my appetite. I'd long ago learned to separate the crimes of mankind from my eating habits. It was why I had to work out regularly, to keep from becoming overweight. Time spent with silverware didn't burn much fat.

"Anything more you can tell me?" I asked after enjoying a few bites and starting on my second beer.

17

"He has a team of thugs," stated Brandon after swallowing down half his meal. "When the going gets too difficult for his team, he brings in a man named Wolfe. I don't know much about him or his last name. Word is he is tough, mean and deadly—an assassin for hire. Seems to be a bit of a ghost though, as there isn't a whole lot of information on him we've been able to gather. He is on the move a lot, working wherever the money leads him. When things get messy, Powers hires him to put an end to any troubles in a most deadly way."

I groaned, not liking what I was hearing. He would be a foe I didn't care to face.

"Any idea if he is in town?"

"None."

"Description?"

"Large, athletic and black. That's about all I'm privy to."

"It wasn't one of the two guys I encountered today. But if he was as tough as you said, I doubt a woman would have kicked his ass. These are probably local guys they figured were tough enough."

"Since they weren't, tougher may be coming."

Brandon said it with a smile, before returning to his food. I though didn't smile and decided to take the leftovers for later, as my appetite had waned over what I was hearing. When the horrors of the world came knocking on *my* door, it did, after all, quell my appetite.

Chapter 4

With darkness setting in, I decided to visit where Parker and many of the other homeless in the area were taking up refuge. It was an old abandoned manufacturing building south of where I lived, just west of Broadway. The night air wasn't as cold as it had been, but still hovered around freezing. When I got there, I planned to carry my leftovers with me to offer them up to Parker, or anyone else who wanted them.

Pulling in I saw the same large black Ford SUV parked outside that carried the two men who had caused the scene at the Mission, both anger and concern at their presence filling me. I pulled out my cell phone and made a call to Denver Police. It was just after shift change, so I had missed getting a hold of Bill Malone and ended up talking with dispatch.

"What can I help you with?" said the woman on the other end.

"I need you to send some officers to this location," I stated, while giving her the approximate address, since I didn't know it. "Used to be the old food manufacturing plant but is now closed."

"What is going on?"

"Two men are here, I believe, to cause trouble. They were at the Mission of the Invisible Souls earlier today making a scene which the police made a report on."

"If the plant is closed, what problems would they be causing?"

"There are homeless people living here. I believe they want to harass them."

"You witnessed them doing this?"

I hesitated. I didn't want to lie but wondered if they'd send someone if I didn't.

"I've not seen them causing trouble yet, but I'm certain it's happening because of a source I have. His name is Parker Turner."

"Is he available for me to talk with to confirm the issue?"

I frowned while mouthing a couple of curse words. "No, he is one of those that are inside being harassed."

"One of the homeless men?"

"Yes."

There was a long pause and I knew I wasn't going to get a good answer, which aggravated me. It truly was hard to get the police to react when it came to the homeless, much like Parker had stated when we first met.

"I will try to get someone out there, but we just had a shift change and its rush hour with more pressing matters."

"Fine!" I said, while hanging up.

You can't slam a cell phone down as convincingly as a desk phone, but I still wanted to smash it for effect. It became clear it was up to me to deal with the issue.

I got out of the Mustang, leaving the food on the seat, a large Maglite flashlight in hand I kept in the car for emergencies, and headed towards the entrance, or what was left of it. I didn't have my gun with me, so it was a matter of me against them. I hoped they weren't packing heat. Though the flashlight was heavy and made a good club, it was no match for a firearm.

I slid inside, eerie darkness filling the space, trepidation invading my nerve endings. I heard threatening voices that concerned me and moved towards them, keeping the light down, tracing my steps, trying not to trample on the garbage and waste that littered the ground. The place smelled damp and sour, as you'd expect an old building would. Down a dingy hallway, past a couple of rats, I came to an open area, where there was some light from a fire burning, the smoke hovering above like a dense shadow. The yelling was louder and I saw one of the two men who were at the Mission pushing around a figure.

"You're going to come with us you ungrateful bastard, or else!" he yelled.

It was bright enough that I could see it was Parker and he wasn't backing down. The man tried to grab him, but Parker took a step in and punched the guy in the face. It didn't put him down, but did draw blood, which he spat on the littered surface. Now angry, he reached into his coat and pulled out a five-inch knife and lunged, stabbing Parker in the stomach before he could react. He keeled over letting out a large groan and dropped to his knees, after the assailant pulled out the blade.

During the confrontation I ran towards them, yelling out in shock at the violent action, but was too late to stop the knifing. His partner stepped over and tried to cut me off. With the butt end of the flashlight, I clubbed him in the head and he went down. I then faced the one with the knife. He was the shaved-headed one Sam had slammed to the table, though he didn't have a knife at the time. Blood dripped from the blade as he gazed at me. I could see fear and a touch of craziness in his eyes. He knew what he'd done was stupid, but now he had me to face and he wasn't about to get arrested, determined to do whatever it took. But I wasn't about to let him get away either.

The knife was in his left hand and he wildly swung it at me from his right to left, then back left to right, taking a couple of passes, missing each time. Gauging his movements, I swung downward with the butt end of the flashlight, timing it perfectly and cracked him on the wrist. He yelped and dropped the knife, clutching at the injured appendage with his other hand in pain. I then stepped in and clocked him with a solid left that rattled his jaw and dropped him to the ground.

I heard a sound behind me and turned, but his partner was running away for the second time that day, leaving his cohort behind. I kicked at his friend but he didn't move. I then went over to Parker hoping to find him still breathing.

"Parker, hang in there," I said while calling 911. This time I got their attention, and paramedics and police were on their way.

"Damn it hurts," moaned Parker, clutching at his stomach.

He was bleeding badly, so I pulled off my gloves and used them to put pressure on his wound. I then stripped my coat off and covered him as best as I could.

"Help is on the way," I declared. "Don't give up on me, soldier."

I think I saw a small smile, as he closed his eyes. I wasn't sure he was going to make it until the paramedics stepped in and took over when they arrived a few minutes later. They got him stabilized before putting him on a gurney, all the while asking him questions he was responding to.

"Where are you taking him?" I queried.

"Swedish Medical Center."

"Parker, I will stop by and visit once I'm done talking with the police," I said while grabbing his hand.

He gave me a thumbs up which was a good sign. As they wheeled him away, I went back to the officers who had the bald man on the ground. They hadn't cuffed him yet, as another set of paramedics were now tending to his injuries. Apparently not only had I broken his nose, I'd done the same to his wrist. He was doing a lot of groaning, which I didn't feel at all guilty about.

One of the police officers on the scene was April Rainn, who I'd been spending a lot of personal time with these last few months. She filled out her dark blue officer uniform nicely, looking sharp, her brown hair pulled up and pinned in back. She looked at me and smiled.

"Do you need a jacket?" she asked, noticing I wasn't draped in one.

I'd been ramped up, so I hadn't felt the cold at first, but now I did, as the adrenaline wore off.

"Your smile is warmth enough," I replied with a forced grin. "Though I wouldn't turn down a blanket."

She got one from one of the paramedics and wrapped it around me, giving me a small hug in the process.

"What are you into now?" she inquired, knowing full well the line of work I was in, and the trouble I'd been known to gravitate to.

"I wish I knew completely," I answered, and then proceeded to explain what happened and what brought me here.

"There seems to be a few other homeless people wandering around," noted April. "Since this is now an active crime scene they can't stay here."

"Can we get transport to The Mission of the Invisible Souls? They will put them up for now."

"I'll see what I can do. Maybe we can get a bus of some type to load them into. But it may take some time and we'll need to talk with them. Many though are leery of us. Since you came to the rescue of their cohort, maybe they will talk with you."

Maybe they would. I wasn't one of them, but possibly close enough. Either way I planned to fight for them and figure out what the hell was going on. I walked over, putting out my hand and did my best to make contact.

Chapter 5

Making the rounds, I found eighteen people living in the abandoned building. Most were males, but I did run across two females. Many of them shied away from me and wouldn't talk, hiding in their makeshift homes of cardboard, old blankets, and an occasional polyester waterproof tent. A couple of people did come out and talk, wondering what would become of them. I assured them the Mission would provide shelter until the situation was resolved.

One of the men came up to me curious about Parker's condition. He was a tall black man, wearing a heavy hooded coat, his hands buried deep in the pockets trying to stay warm. I put out my hand and he shook it, though quickly and gently, before tucking it back away.

"His wound was bad, but they think he'll pull though," I declared. "Do you know Parker?"

"Yes," he replied, softly. "I guess you would say we were friends."

"Did you see and hear what happened? How it all started."

He glanced around nervous to answer.

"Don't worry they won't find out you said anything. I promise." I took my index finger and made an X on my chest.

Weighing his words, he finally commented.

"Those two guys were trying to lure everyone away. Flashing hundred-dollar bills if we'd come with them. Said more where that came from, if we got in their vehicle."

"You didn't believe them?"

He glanced around, still nervous about talking. "Parker didn't and that was good enough for me. Good enough for many around here. They had been by before taking people away. Then we never see them again. Parker didn't trust them and made it clear to those who would listen. He'd grown tired of their lies, standing up to them, and telling them to leave the rest of us alone. The bald guy got angry and tried to force him to go. That's when Parker hit him, and the guy stuck him with what appeared to be a knife."

"Yes, I saw that part. I wished I'd gotten there a couple minutes earlier. I might have been able to stop the stabbing." I sighed, unhappy I couldn't intervene sooner.

"You took them both out like it was nothing," noted the man, sounding impressed.

"I do this for a living and they were amateurs. I'm a private detective. Parker asked me to look into what was going on around here."

He sized me up with his eyes, before nodding.

"I wondered if you were him. Parker had mentioned he'd talked to a PI. Looked like you had some training. Parker was in the military, as was I. He though had more field experience than I did. I was wounded early in my tour and couldn't go back. Lots of my fellow soldiers died the day I was hurt." He paused, sadness lacing his face. "Since then I've shied away from confrontation. I feel bad I didn't come to help him too."

"Where did you see combat?" I asked.

"Iraq and Kuwait. The first war there. Parker was there too, though we didn't serve together."

"I'm sorry your country isn't taking better care of you," I noted with concern in my tone.

"They tried for a while, the VA did. But government funding and personnel cuts, and it wasn't long before many of us were forgotten." His voice got shaky. "It was hard for me to work…because I still feel like I'm there at times…in the middle of the battle zone. I can't shake the pain of my wounds…the deaths of others around me…on that fateful day."

His words reminded me of what Sam had stated, about those haunting times consuming her. And how they still haunted her, but now she accepted the pain, allowing herself to feel bad without being paralyzed by it. An emotion many soldiers strived for but never reached, much like this man before me.

"You were diagnosed with PTSD?"

He nodded, the shaky emotion under control. "Yes. The VA provided counseling to work through it. And some drugs helped, but I couldn't afford them without their assistance. When they wouldn't cover it anymore, I relapsed. In time, I ended up on the streets, as I was unable to hold a job. Some days are better than others, though my dreams are often laced with the war-torn events. Parker understood, having lived in much of it and could relate to what I was internalizing. I'm afraid I may never see him again."

24

It was a shame the VA hadn't continued to help him. Stories of the huge cost overruns of over a billion of dollars for the new, but still not open, VA hospital in Aurora, while soldiers who had fought for their country were being left out in the cold. It was a wrong doing the politicians and bureaucrats would pledge to fix, but never got around to. While their pay and benefits marched merrily on and their sterile cushy freshly painted and leather furnished offices they occupied, sat completely walled off and far away from the battle zones. Many had never even served or received deferments, thanks to their family's wealth.

"I plan to help as best as I can," I said. "Parker will be back in time. I guarantee it. Right now, we need to learn more about these guys so we can put them away for hurting him. And then get you all somewhere to stay while the police work the scene. I believe the Mission of the Invisible Souls can put every one of you up for the foreseeable future. Can you help me talk with the others? Convince them to come with us."

He looked down at his boots, uncertain what to say. He then turned around and saw all the people behind him, many of which were agitated with what was happening. The police, paramedics and now even the press were there. The majority of them just wishing the throng of people would all go away and leave them in peace. But that wasn't going to happen.

"You can help them…give us a safe place to stay?" he inquired.

"Yes. Many won't talk with me. But they may listen to you."

He nodded his head.

"I'm Jarvis. What is your name?"

"Call me T. That's what the others know me as."

"Lead the way, T. I'm at your service."

He turned and walked towards the others. I stayed a step behind so as not to spook any of them. We made the rounds and slowly were able to get most on board with leaving. A couple still weren't convinced, and we didn't want to force them. They finally agreed when I showed them pictures of the Mission on my phone. We told them to grab a few necessary items and be ready to go.

April had arranged for an RTD bus to transport everyone. T and I rode up front and helped lead everyone into the building. There were several volunteers there to guide and help. Hot food and blankets were provided, with cots set up in the overflow area on the first floor providing a place for them to sleep. It took maybe an hour to get the group settled. I told T I'd be back tomorrow to talk, but I needed to check on Parker and learn more about his attacker. I walked out feeling I'd made some significant progress, though there was much work still ahead. The adrenaline was still pumping, but I was running on empty. I decided to go home, crawl in bed and sleep, so I could battle on the next day.

Chapter 6

I enjoyed a restful night of sleep, feeling recharged and ready to go. There was much work ahead of me, needing all the energy I could muster, now fueled by a scrambled egg and sausage breakfast with orange juice to drink, purchased at the nearby drive thru.

After satisfying my stomach, I drove down to Denver Police Headquarters to check on the arrested attacker of Parker. He'd been taken to the hospital but should have been in custody by now.

When I arrived, he wasn't there, having already been bailed out by some high-end lawyers. My Denver PD contact, Bill Monroe, filled me in on the details as I stood next to his paperwork littered desk.

"Some bigwigs from the east coast. Flew in on a private jet from what I heard. They had him out of here by 8 a.m. this morning."

How this low-life got an Armani suited legal team to bail him out was telling. It would appear they were connected. And connected people have powerful organizations pulling the strings, which only confirmed my suspicions a major player was involved.

"Did the detectives grill him for information on who hired him before they arrived?"

Bill frowned at me. "Do you think the detectives walk over to my desk and spill everything that happens in the interrogation room?"

I smiled back at his grumpy words. "They love you, Bill. I think they share all their deep and darkest secrets with you."

Bill shook his head in disbelief. "We may need to drug test you to find out what you've been smoking, Jarvis."

I laughed. "Come on, I know you hear much of what goes on around here. Certainly, there was water cooler talk about what the detectives did and if they learned anything."

Bill sighed, looked around and whispered. "You didn't hear it from me. They *did* question him, and he didn't say a word. That is when counsel showed up and put an end to the interrogation."

"Do you have the name of the firm?"

Bill gave me another angry glance.

"Worth beers and dinner at Boone's."

"Why are you working this?" Bill inquired.

"The man who was stabbed is my client."

Leaning back in his chair, Bill appeared surprised. "From what I understand the man who was injured is homeless. I doubt he'll be paying you for your services any time soon."

"I'm doing it out of the goodness of my heart. My Christmas present to the world," I stated gleefully.

Bill huffed a few more times before leaning forward, typing on his keyboard to find the information.

"Krieg & Williamson. Stationed out of New York City."

Getting the proper spelling, I typed the name down in my phone, saying thank you, before being waved off so he could return to the mound of paperwork that wouldn't improve his mood any.

There wasn't anything more I could do here, so I decided to go to the Swedish Medical Center to check on Parker. When I arrived, he'd been transferred to a private room. He'd had surgery to close his wound and to make sure there was no major internal damage. It had been a serious injury, with significant blood loss, but it looked as if he would recover if there were no complications.

When I got to his room, I knocked on the door. There was no response, so I stuck my head in. He was asleep, so I strolled in quietly and found a chair to sit in. I pulled out my phone, logged into the hospital Wi-Fi and did some research.

Krieg & Williamson was indeed out of New York, with an office in one of the expensive Manhattan skyrises. They dealt with any type of legal cases but specialized in corporate law. It seemed odd they would fly out to take on a stabbing case for a nobody that worked for Boss Builders, until I saw the list of some of their major clients. Liquid Investors was near the top, as was Powers USA Inc.

In my mind this was certainly a clue and an important one, providing me more confirmation, for both would qualify as major players. The website didn't lead me anywhere else but did provide a phone number. I entered it in my phone contacts, to reference later.

I then looked up Powers USA Inc and found they were from New Jersey, though with offices in many major cities east of the

Mississippi. There was a bio pic of the founder and CEO, Tyrell Powers. It said he was forty-eight years old and had gone to Yale University where he received his various business degrees. The bio went on to say he'd built his business on perseverance and smart investments. Not surprisingly there was no mention of any criminal tendencies in his endeavors. The picture showed a handsome black man, with dark jacket and open neck lavender shirt. His glimmering ivory smile looked forced and hardly natural. From what Brandon had said about his shark-like nature, this was hardly surprising.

"Where am I?" I heard Parker croak.

I stood up, moving next to his bed. It was good to see him coming around.

"You're in a room at the Swedish Medical Center. You had surgery because you were stabbed."

Parker's eyes were open, closed and then open again. He was having a hard time focusing. I was certain he was on some heavy pain drugs. He tried to sit up, but I put my hand on his shoulder to keep him from moving too far. I heard his bed alarm go off and a nurse hustled into the room to check on him.

"Please don't move too much," she said while checking his bandages. "You don't want to tear open any of those stitches. You had a deep stab wound." She stopped to look at me. "Who are you?"

"A friend. I was there when he was attacked. I'm also a private detective." I showed her my ID.

Glancing at it, she didn't seem impressed. "Do you know this man, Parker?" she queried.

Parker's eyes started to clear some. He looked my way and nodded. "Jarvis?"

I smiled, happy he remembered.

"Talk with him and keep him relaxed," ordered the nurse. "Are you in pain, Parker?"

It took him a few seconds to answer. "Yes."

"What is your pain level from one to ten?"

He thought about it for a minute. "Eight."

"Let me see what we can get you."

She stepped out of the room to check with a doctor. I stood beside the bed and softly put my hand back on his shoulder.

"You're doing great," I noted. "Much better than last night. Do you remember what happened?"

He nodded again. "Asshole knifed me."

I grinned. "Aptly described. He was arrested. I also broke his nose and wrist if it makes you feel any better."

He winced. "Not really, but good to know he didn't get away with it."

"I talked with T and he told me all that happened."

He gave a small, painful nod. "Same guys I told you about before. Though more aggressive since the rest of us weren't buying their story."

The nurse returned with some pills and water, which she handed to him to take.

"Hungry," he said after swallowing them down.

"Probably can get you some soup. Only liquids for a few days."

"Chicken noodle?" Parker said hopefully.

She smiled. "I think we can arrange that. Though broth only for now."

As she left, I thought over what to bring up. I didn't want to get him too upset but I needed to learn more about him and what happened. I knew he was a soldier, now out on the streets with nothing but the clothes on his back and what fit in his shopping cart. He would require help going forward. The medical bills would be through the roof. I imagined we could get the VA and the parties responsible to help, with some legal wrangling on my part.

"What branch of service were you in?" I asked.

"Army."

"You were injured?"

"Shrapnel in the leg from an anti-personnel mine. Took some time to heal, but I was back fighting again once I recovered. I was the lucky one though, others around me were killed, having took the brunt of the shrapnel."

"Do you feel you were lucky?"

His reaction remained sterile. "Not really. There are days when I wished I'd died."

There were times I wondered why I had survived some of the battles I'd been through. *Why do some live, while others around you perish?* It was the million-dollar question no one had answers to.

30

"You survived for a reason. I'm sure of it. In this case helping your homeless companions and bringing me into the fray. Maybe we can help all of you find your way."

"How so?"

"We're going to get those involved to pay up. I have a friend who can take action."

"Who?"

The timing was good. In walked Barry Anders, my lawyer, who was a pain in the ass, but an excellent litigator. Dressed casually for him; dark jeans, golf shirt and tennis shoes, he smiled with leather-bound briefcase in hand. I had called, and after the usual moaning from him, wondering what I needed, he agreed after I explained in detail the circumstances. He sounded excited about the possibility of where it could lead. Big paydays always got him raring to go.

"Mr. Turner, I'm Barry Anders. I'm a lawyer who would like to help you out, if you'll let me."

Parker turned his head carefully, a grim expression on his face. "I'm homeless with nothing to pay you."

"Not a problem. I will work for a percentage of the settlement, per a discounted rate at Jarvis' urging. It won't cost you a nickel."

"What settlement?"

"Hopefully a big one," Barry announced with complete joy in his tone. "Money that will allow you to get back on your feet."

"Why would you do this?" wondered Parker, disbelief on his face.

"Because Jarvis asked me. And I'm sucker for those in need."

He seemed surprised and moved by the words.

"Thank you...both of you," he said while choking up.

"If you're up to it, I'd like for you to tell me everything, from the beginning."

He nodded yes and Barry pulled out a digital recorder, pressing the start button.

"Start with how you were injured in Iraq and we'll work from there."

Parker took a deep breath and told us his story.

Chapter 7

I live a life where danger haunts me. People were often trying to kill me or kill those I loved. They had been successful in killing my brother and I'd been injured myself, though nothing life threatening. But listening to Parker and his description of each day on the battlefield, where the enemy's sole purpose was to kill you, made for a scary vision. Bullets flying at you from all directions. Missiles and bombs falling from the sky from fighter jets or unmanned drones, with little or no warning. Mines and IUD's hidden in the dirt, and sand—a danger to the foot soldier or the vehicles they travelled in. Teetering on the edge of death nearly every minute of the day.

A soldier's existence was a hairy one. A life I wasn't sure I could live. It took another type of bravery, one you'd reach deep down to achieve, to step out and face that challenge. One could see where it could leave a man feeling broken and unwanted. No man left behind was a motto you often heard. In reality, many had been left behind with little or nothing of value to cling to.

When Barry had gathered all he needed, he assured Parker he would do everything he could to help. We left him to the nurses, doctors and his chicken broth, promising to return. I even said I'd bring T by so they could talk.

I took a couple of days to think through my next options. Asking myself the question of where I could go now to learn more, to find out who was behind all of this. It could have been random, but there was little evidence I'd seen that was the case. The major players were Boss Builders, Liquid Investors and Powers USA Inc. I decided to start where the two assailants worked and looked up Boss Builders. They had an office in Denver, north of I25, on Federal and 88th street.

I jumped in the Mustang and headed north, navigating the city roads and traffic. The weather was colder today, and it felt like snow might be coming in. I cranked the heat up on high, along with some driving music to help pass the time and warm the flesh.

When I arrived, the place looked closed. There were construction trucks, and others similar to the Ford the two assailants had been driving. Some were labeled with the company name, others weren't. The main entrance was locked, a sign up saying they had closed and gone out of business. No date of when this happened was displayed.

I called the main number and it played a message saying the same thing. Any business inquiries were to be made with Liquid Investors, along with a number to call. When I called those digits, I got another recording, saying much the same, but you could leave a message and someone would get back with you within twenty-four hours. Which I did, saying I was an angry client whose work hadn't been completed and that I'd be suing for damages if the project wasn't finished ASAP. Leaving no details other than my cell number, I used my stern voice, the one that made gangsters drop their guns in fear and suck their thumbs.

As I sat outside, I thought over my next course of action. If the closing coincided with the attack and arrest, they could be covering their tracks. Of course, big investment companies buy businesses every day and shut them down, as the assets were worth more than the business they were doing. I could go right up and ask Liquid Investors directly, but I doubted they would share what their business plan was all along for Boss Builders. While contemplating the merits of paying them a visit, my phone rang. It was Bill.

"The bald knife wielder never showed for his hearing today," he said. "We've got an address and I'm heading out to bring him in. You up for coming along?"

Bill normally didn't do much other than work behind a desk, because of a past injury that left him in pain. But today apparently was different.

"Nothing better than a ride along," I quipped.

"I'm the senior officer and we're shorthanded. Figured you'd be happy to break his other wrist if given the chance. And I'd be happy to have the backup."

"Put me in coach," I replied. "Are you going to deputize me?"

He blurted out a few curse words before giving me the address, which was halfway between us. I told him I'd meet him there with the promise I wouldn't do anything until he arrived.

It took about twenty minutes to get there, the apartment in a rundown neighborhood in West Denver. Once parked, I pulled out my .38, sat and waited, singing along to my rock playlist. Bill showed about five minutes later in his Denver PD black & white.

We made a beeline towards the apartment office to get a key. The manager didn't want to hand over anything until Bill showed him the arrest warrant he was possessing. The manager reluctantly called the maintenance man with the master key, who took us to the second-floor room. The hallway was dark and dirty, smelling as if animals lived and defecated there.

He gave us a quick rundown of the layout of the space. Living area, kitchen, and down the hall a bathroom and two small bedrooms. Bill asked him to step back while he knocked on the door, his gun holster unsnapped.

"Blaine Mason, this is the Denver Police," he announced after pounding several times. It was the first time I'd heard the name. "We have a warrant for your arrest. Open the door or we'll open it."

Bill kept his body away from the entrance in case someone tried to fire through it. After a couple of minutes, he had the maintenance man unlock it.

"Please go down the hall and stay there," Bill demanded. "Jarvis, are you ready?"

I said yes, with my .38 in hand, prepared to follow. My adrenaline was flowing, knowing the man was capable of violence. Bill had his gun out as he opened the door and glanced around the corner watching for any danger. He didn't see anything and stepped in, and I was a foot behind. No one was in the living area, which consisted of an old green fabric couch, heavily worn brown recliner, and old tube TV. The kitchen area was to the left with table and two chairs, noisy refrigerator and gas stove. Bill had his gun up, watching for any movement. There was no balcony, so the only place left they could be was down the hall, to the bedrooms or bath.

"Blaine," Bill yelled out again. "This is the Denver Police. If you're home, you need to come out now."

No answer and the place was strangely quiet. It was also cold, with a smell I'd encountered before. And not a good smell.

"You smell that?" I asked Bill.

"Yea. I think I know what we'll find at the end of the hall."

All the remaining doors were closed and Bill led the way. The first was the bathroom, which he opened, stepping in. Nothing was inside, and it smelled like you'd expect a dirty bathroom would smell like. At the end were two more doors. The closer we got the worse the smell. Bill opened the first door to find what we expected.

The body was dead, lying on the bed. Eyes and mouth open, as if surprised. There was vomit on his chin, neck and shirt, but no blood. Blaine had died from something, though we didn't know what.

When opening the second door, we found another body, much the same. This was his partner, the one who had fled the scene. He was on his side, the shirt-less body half off the bed, as if he had struggled to get up, a shocked expression on his dirty face. They had likely been dead for many hours. The question would be what had killed them. It didn't appear they'd been shot or beaten.

Bill got on his radio and called it in. Within fifteen minutes the place was crawling with cops, including Detective Mallard. The coroner arrived and placed the time of death at some time the previous day. His first impression was poisoning. The other possibly was a drug overdose. After some searching there were drugs and paraphernalia found. The question was, did they do it to themselves or did someone do it to them?

"I'll need a few days for a toxicology screening to confirm," declared the coroner.

"Put a rush on it," proclaimed Mallard. "We need to find out what happened here. If it's a homicide, then there are many questions we'll need answered.

When he said those last words, Mallard looked directly at me. All I could do was shrug. But in my heart, I knew it wasn't accidental. Someone didn't want these two to talk. Something bigger than pushing around homeless people was going on here.

Chapter 8

The next day Sam made arrangements for me to meet with the church who owned the Mission. The Holy Blood Catholic Church was a mile or so west of the shelter, in a slightly more upscale neighborhood of half-million-dollar homes.

The church structure was designed of classic architecture; two-stories of charcoal-gray brick walls, with a bell tower and large white cross gracing the center of the pitched roof of terracotta shingles, across a huge lot, with numerous hundred-year-old cotton wood trees taller than the main structure. With a modern multi-room school in a separate building and offices in another, I walked the cobblestone path to the matching charcoal-gray brick offices to meet with the man in charge, Father Francis.

Once inside I was escorted to his office by an older fifties-aged woman, who may have been a nun, but was dressed today in a black pants suit. She offered me coffee, tea or water, which I gracefully declined, before leaving me alone, after she explained the Father would be along in a matter of minutes.

The entire space was rectangular, the ceiling twelve-foot-high, mostly to accommodate the towering bookshelf that took nearly most of one wall, with too many books to count filling the shelves from top to bottom. Two large spinning fans hung from the ceiling, a pair of tinted skylights allowing the rays of the sun to filter in on this crisp cloudless day.

On the other wall I saw plaques of accomplishments and recognition for the work done here in Colorado by the church and its members. Numerous pictures of church events, sports and fundraisers joined the plaques. Even one of what I assumed was Father Francis with one of the past Catholic Popes, though I had no idea which. And further down one of Sam and the Father, her arm around him with a few of their homeless patrons in the Mission's dining area.

As I made it to the end of the wall of pictures, a door opened and in walked an older man using a cane. He was dressed in a black cassock that flowed to his ankles, with traditional black and white clerical collar adorning his neck. His gray hair was cut short, dwindling on the top, with a combover that did little to hide the thinning. He moved slowly, each step deliberate, the quad walking cane in his right hand keeping him balanced. He ambled over to me, nearly my height as we were eye to eye, holding out his hand, embracing mine softly for several minutes. Introducing himself, he told me to have a seat on the red velvet sofa in the middle of the room, as he sat next to me.

"I understand, Jarvis, you're a private detective," noted Father Francis with an engaging smile.

"I am, Father. Been my profession for many years now."

"Most interesting, and please, call me Francis. I hate the formality when we're chatting socially." He grinned ear to ear, making me feel at ease. "I'm sure you deal with the seedy side of life. What is that like?"

"Challenging, but at times fulfilling, when I'm able to help a client out of a bad situation."

"Leading them out of the darkness and into the light can be wonderful. Much as we try to do every day around here."

"I'm not always successful, though," I commented with a frown.

His smile waned. "Neither are we, son. Though we try—we can't save everyone."

I nodded my head, knowing he spoke the truth, though it still hurts when you fail. I'd seen misery and death more times than I cared to admit. The successes tipped the scale, but only slightly.

"You have quite an impressive wall of pictures," I stated, while pointing at them. "Even one with you and the Pope. Where was that taken?"

He grinned. "Here in Denver when Pope John Paul II visited back in 1993. What a tremendous day for us and the city. The crowd for him at Cherry Creek State Park was like that of a rock star. Around 800,000 attended."

I was too young to remember that event. And even if I did, I was a teenager living in Des Moines at the time. For that many people to show up, would have been incredible. I wasn't a religious man per se, but I would have been inclined to join the masses gathering for a day of peaceful reflection.

"How long have you known Pastor Sam?" he inquired.

"We only met recently. But I was most impressed with the facility and doubly so with her. She is quite a woman."

"She is a godsend and makes it all work there," he said while crossing himself and putting his hands together. "We had many issues until she took over and assembled the solid staff she has. Her strict rules about what is and isn't allowed has made it a shrine for people out on the streets in need. If only I could clone her, though that might be counterman to the lord's wishes."

He laughed at his own humor, causing me to smile.

"Sam told me you had some questions about The Mission of the Invisible Souls," he queried.

"I understand someone has made an offer to buy the building. I'm curious if you can enlighten me about this offer."

His eyebrows rose to my question. "Possibly. Though I would need to understand the reason why you're asking."

I often would exaggerate or withhold the truth when doling out information. In this case, being where I was and who I was talking with, I figured it was best to give all the facts.

"It has come to my attention someone has been moving homeless people out of this area, using money to bribe them and in some cases when that doesn't work, forcefully remove them. One man was stabbed two days ago when he refused their offer."

"Oh that is horrible," he replied, his body quivering at the words. "What is the reason behind why they are trying to move these poor souls?"

"I'm not certain yet. That is why I'm asking the question about the offer. Investigating, I traced back to a couple of companies who might be involved in the threats. I wanted to see if any of these names are who've been in contact with you."

Father Francis thought it over for a minute, rubbing a gold cross and crucifix on a chain in his hand he'd removed from his pocket before responding. "The buyers asked to keep the offer in confidence. We agreed to this, but in light of what you're telling me, if you throw out names, I can deny the ones who aren't involved, but won't confirm the ones that are."

Sneaky little devil, though I didn't tell him this.

"Fair enough. What about Boss Builders?"

"No."

"Liquid Investors?"

He shook his head.

"Powers USA Inc?"

Again, his response was no. I was running out of names, before I thought of one other, which I had to look up on my phone to make sure I said it correctly.

"A law firm from back east…Krieg & Williamson?"

This time he didn't say anything, remaining silent as if I hadn't uttered a word. It would seem the law firm was handling the sale. Shielding their clients from prying eyes, using client confidentiality to protect them, at least in the initial process.

"How was the offer then in terms of a dollar amount?" I queried, hunting for more details.

Again he thought for a moment, still rubbing the cross.

"I will say it was a lowball amount they offered. Basically the value of the land but nothing else. It sounded as if their plan was to bulldoze the structure and rebuild."

"And what was your response?"

"A flat no, so they upped the offer. But we aren't in this to make a profit. We're there to help people in need."

I was making progress. More clues to the puzzle, which was shining a light on what was going on.

"And what would happen if the need dwindled or diminished completely?"

He appeared surprised by the question, a perplexed expression on his face. "I'm not certain what you mean?"

"Let's say there is no more homeless in the area to serve. The need of shelter for them goes away and you have an empty or near empty building you no longer have a purpose for."

He lowered his head, contemplating, before speaking.

"Though I pray every day for this to come true, I doubt the homeless situation will go away in my lifetime. There will always be a need."

"Certainly, there will be. But this goes to what I'm hearing is happening. Moving the homeless out of this area to who knows where. There still is a need, but not where the Mission is located. You might be willing to sell to them, and possibly take that money to an area where now there is a bigger need."

"You believe that is what is happening here?" he wondered.

I shrugged. "I don't have all the answers. But the name I gave last works for two of those other companies I mentioned, one of which has a history of doing what it takes to acquire the property

39

they desire by any means necessary, including practices not becoming of God loving people."

Father Francis slowly stood up, using his cane to balance himself and began a careful saunter, my words appearing to disturb him. He reached his desk, looking up at a life-sized statue of Jesus Christ dressed in flowing white gown and holding a Bible in his hand. After several minutes he turned around, walking back over to where I was standing, the two of us eye to eye.

"It never ceases to amaze me how the mighty dollar can poison people to do horrible things, if what you say is true." He put a hand on my shoulder. "You're a strong, confident, proud man. I can see this clearly from how you speak and hold yourself. Is it your intention to stop what is happening to these poor people?"

"Absolutely," I stated with an air of confidence and pride. "I will do what it takes and put an end to it, once I'm certain what is going on."

Father Francis' face beamed with joy. "I'm not certain if you were looking for it, but you have my blessing to find these men and stop them. These poor people need to be left in peace. They have been through enough and deserve better."

"Thank you, Father. You can rest assured I will get to the bottom of this."

He removed his hand. "God bless you. If it's any consolation we had no intention of selling to them, no matter what evil they attempt, or the dollar amount they throw at us. There is a higher calling here that we'll continue to follow to help those in need." He stood beside me, putting his arm through mine. "If that is all, I will see you to the door, for I have much work to do. I've enjoyed our chat and hopefully you'll stop by when you get to the bottom of this mess and tell me all about it."

I nodded as he led me to the door, where he turned to hold my hand, cupping it with both of his.

"You mentioned this poor homeless man who was stabbed was your client. It leads me to believe you aren't being paid for your services. It's quite noble you doing this out of the goodness of your heart."

"Thank you. A little gesture where I can give something back, for I've not always walked the ethical path the Almighty would want me on."

"You're not alone, my son," he said with a smile, before I walked away knowing the mission I was on was a righteous one.

Chapter 9

Several days had passed, and I was at a standstill. I tried contacting Krieg & Williamson, but never received a call back, even though the receptionist claimed she'd pass on a message. No response from Liquid Investors from the message I left about Boss Builders. It would seem no one wanted to talk to a gumshoe about this situation, which angered me.

The crime scene of the two dead men had revealed no clues beyond guesses. The deaths were suspicious, the results still forthcoming from the coroner. Christmas was fourteen days away and I wanted a viable solution before the holidays. Since the bald man and his partner were dead, there was no crime anymore for the police to investigate when it came to the stabbing.

The old abandoned building was now open again for the homeless to go back to, their stuff still there. After encouragement from me, T was going to watch after things as best as he could. The question I asked myself—was the attempt to move the homeless out of the space over now? There was no reason to believe that their plan was complete, for the objective still existed for getting them out of there, whatever it may be. I needed to learn what their true motives were.

Every idea that came to mind led me to the same conclusion. I needed to join the homeless, to become one of them. I'd let my facial hair grow out and went to a thrift store to find some old worn-out clothing to blend in. I planned to live among them and see what I could discover.

My first day in their world was a tough one. I wasn't used to surviving in the cold, wind and snow for hours at a time. You learned to move around as much as you could, to keep the blood flowing. T helped to keep me focused, telling me tricks he used to make it more bearable. Using trees, walls and any type of solid structures as barriers to the frosty wind. Locating heat sources like vents of exhaust from buildings and even from grates built in the ground where you could find warmer air rising. I did have my cell phone and gun, in case I needed it, as well as packaged food and water to get me by. But I was trying to live as much as they lived, wandering among them, trying to blend in.

When it got late, close to midnight, I did go back to my place and slept. I knew I couldn't sleep in these conditions. *How did they do it?* I could barely make it to the fifteen-hour mark without going insane. They lived this way every second of the day, with little or nothing, other than what they were able to obtain from handouts. No one should ever have to survive this way. Yet tens of thousands across our great country did. It was hard to feel great living in such a rich society as ours when so many had so little. It was the definition of human suffering before my eyes.

To help pass the time, I made the rounds and tried to communicate with the others, with T's help. Most were still leery and wanted little to do with me. Others were more accommodating. I'd bring some extra food and water, handing out some mostly as a peace offering. Over the days, I got to know a little about a few of them. Some through personal interaction and conversation, and others via T.

I learned a little about CJ, one of the two females living on the local streets. She loved items with the US Flag on them, wearing caps, shirts and even patches on her jacket. The irony of this not lost upon me. She had come to the streets when the medical facility she was staying in ran out of funds to treat her illness. Tourette syndrome was her malady, a neuropsychiatric disorder she'd had since childhood. Her illness had progressively gotten worse with age, where early in her life, she had learned to control it without medication.

When other mental health issues started affecting her, the symptoms became worse, including paranoia, ADHD and OCD, requiring full-time care. But she had no insurance and couldn't work, so no medical facility long-term would foot the bill to care for her. There was no family, at least anyone with money to help, so she was out on the streets, fending for herself these last few months. She was doing her best, but one could see the toll it took. She spent a lot of time talking to herself; swearing, yelling, her movements at times shaky and uncontrolled. Other times she found calmness. I talked with her about her love of the flag.

"The colors," she would say. "Such a beautiful combination." She would look up at the sky, pointing with her gloved hands. "Stars. Twinkle, twinkle."

I glowed at her innocent love of something so simple. "Yes, it's magnificent."

"I find a...peacefulness...if I gaze at it long enough," she said another time.

She wasn't always sure who I was, or why I was there. I gave her no illusions that I could save her, because I doubted I could. But conversing seemed to help, either with me or the others, or to herself. She had fashioned a cardboard home, with sleeping bag and pillow, to rest in, when she could find the peace in her brain to sleep.

One of the others was Laramie. He was a little older than I was, a hard worker, he told me, but had been making barely above minimum wage, previously working two jobs to make ends meet. He had lived in a rundown apartment but was forced out when they sold out to some big investor, who then pushed all the tenants out onto the street. He couldn't find another place he could afford. Housing costs were through the roof and eventually he was living in his car.

Times got tough after losing both jobs in the span of a few months, and he had to sell his car, putting him on the streets, homeless. He'd been tempted to take the cash when the men came around, but he resisted, not trusting them. He told me of hopes of finding his way back to a normal life, wanting to prove to others and to himself he could pull out of this mess, though uncertain how to get there. Once you're down this far, it was nearly impossible to get back up without assistance.

"Thanks," he said when I offered him a granola bar. "Handouts have been slow today. I may need to stop by the Mission to get some food. I haven't eaten much the last couple of days."

"I'm sure they can provide a warm meal," I noted. "It's why they're there—to help."

"Pride gets in the way sometimes," he replied ruefully, showing emotion baring his soul. "You tell yourself you shouldn't have to ask for help. I thought it couldn't happen to me and that being a hard worker was enough to keep me employed. Fate often doesn't care about the effort you make."

"Nothing wrong with pride," I answered. "Pride might be what will drive you to get back on your feet."

He nodded at my words, though I wasn't completely certain he found solace in them.

44

There were others I had spoken to. Each with their own story. Often unique, yet similar in many ways the road that led them here. Sometimes it was of their own doing. Silly mistakes they wished they could turn back time on. Other cases it was drugs, alcohol or illness that brought them down. Or just plain bad luck—or fate as Laramie stated. Blame would fall on others and society, and other times they blamed themselves.

I was living among them, but I wasn't them. Sure, I'd been down and nearly penniless myself, but someone, normally family, always had my back. I had been lucky and fortunate, where they hadn't been.

As nighttime fell with the temperatures, I went back to my warm bed to chase sleep. In the end I hoped to do good by them and make a difference, even in the smallest of ways.

We reached day six, and I was getting tired and frustrated, thinking nothing was coming of the effort I had given. It seemed no end was in sight when I finally got the break I was hoping for.

This time two other hefty men showed up, offering to provide work for anyone who wanted it. They flashed hundred dollar bills and promises of food, clothing and shelter, if we came along. One of the men came up to me with an air of overwhelming confidence. I looked down, trying to appear scared of him. I didn't want to cave too easily.

"You look like you could hold your own," said the pale pockmarked white man to me. "I bet you get tired of being cold and hungry." He reached out with one of the crisp new bills and tried to tuck it in my coat pocket. I backed away.

"Don't be scared," he declared. "We want to help." His words didn't ring sincere.

I mumbled a couple of words he couldn't fathom.

"What?" he asked, holding a hand to his ear.

"I'm cold," I said louder. It wasn't a lie.

"Come into our nice warm SUV. It has heated seats. Hell, I'll even take you to McDonalds and buy you whatever you want. I bet a nice quarter pounder with cheese would hit the spot."

I glanced around, my breathing labored, doing my best acting job to appear scared and uncertain. T was talking with the other guy, a black man with thick, trimmed afro. He was playing it much the same, for we had rehearsed what to do and say.

"I-I don't think...I should. I...d-don't know you." I stammered between pants to add to the effect.

"I'm Bart. What is your name?"

I doubted that was his real name. It didn't matter as I planned on knowing who he was in the end. I paused before answering.

"Smitty."

"Good to meet you, Smitty. Now we know each other."

I continued to not make eye contact. "How m-m-much can I m-m-make?"

"I can give you two hundred now. There is more after you start working. All in cash." His scared face beamed with joy, thinking he had me.

"What do I... n-need to do?"

"Labor. Work with your hands. Can you handle that?"

"Three...hundred?" I said shyly, playing hard to get, while hiding my anger at their manipulating tactic.

He pulled out the money and handed it to me. I held off grabbing it, my hand shaking, partly from acting and partly from the cold, before quickly snagging the cash. I counted it, as if not to trust him. I nodded my head, as if to agree to his terms.

I stood around and waited. We had all agreed that only T and I would go with them. Part of the negotiation would be we would go and if all worked out, we could talk the others into coming along. It was what they wanted. Everyone gone from the property.

After thirty minutes of negotiating, T set the final terms, getting four hundred in cash. We climbed into the back of the SUV, the heated seats nice and warm, and left, not knowing where we were headed.

Once inside, the speeches and sales pitches stopped. The atmosphere of the two men now was as cold as the outdoors, knowing they had us. I checked the back door and we were locked in. I turned and looked at T. He was nervous, anxious to see where we were headed. I nodded while patting his gloved hand, as if to say all would be OK. Though I showed a display of confidence, I was on edge even with my experience in these situations. I knew there was still a chance it could all go sideways and was prepared for the possibility.

"What about McDonalds?" I queried timidly. "Can I get my...quarter pounder plain?"

There was no answer and I saw mocking smiles on their faces after asking, their arrogance aggravating. We drove for thirty minutes and soon were north of the downtown business strip, where a large camp of homeless reside, wandering the streets, the region rundown, many of the buildings in disrepair and abandoned. This appeared to be one of the main homeless cities in the area.

The SUV pulled up and the doors unlocked. The black man on the passenger side turned around and gave us a mean look.

"Get out!" he growled.

"What did you say?" asked T.

"You heard me. I said get your dirty ass out of our vehicle. Ride is over and this is where you live now."

"But what about the job you promised us?" inquired T.

"There is no job. Just need to get you out of our way." His eyes squinted in vile disgust.

"Way of what?" I asked innocently.

"None of your damn business. And you're going to help us get the others to come to, by recording a message on our phone that your new job is great. We need to get the rest of you bums off that land, pronto."

"What if we refuse?" wondered T.

"Then you have a beating coming that you won't enjoy!" He looked genuinely pleased with the prospect of pounding on us.

I looked at T and then pulled my out .38 and pointed it at them.

"I don't think so," I declared. "Today there will be no beatings. Only conversations of who you're working for and why you're dumping people here. Turn off the engine and throw me the keys. Then put your hands on the dash."

They both looked stunned but remained silent. The engine still was running, so I pressed the gun to the driver's short blonde head. He got the message, turning off the motor and tossing the keys back to T.

"Now your guns. You first. Two fingers and slowly hand it back to T."

I'd seen they were carrying when they first arrived. The one on the passenger side hesitated, so I pulled back the hammer, letting him know I meant business before he handed it back, the driver shortly after following suit. T, with his gloved hands, sat them on the seat between us. He knew guns, making certain the safeties were on before laying them down.

"Now either you two start telling me what you're doing and for whom, or we take a walk among these people and let them have at you."

Neither one spoke. Tough guys always took the hardline. It was part of the macho code. But I knew I had time on my side. With T's help, I got them both outside standing in front of the SUV. They remained defiant.

"Remove your coats and gloves," I demanded forcefully.

They both looked at me as if I was insane. It was probably twenty degrees with a significant wind. Even with my layers I was feeling the chill.

"Now, or else!" I said again, waving my gun at them. "I'd hate for this to go off accidentally since my hands are shaking from the cold."

They glanced at each other and finally took off their coats and gloves. One was a nice heavy parka with a hood, the other was brown suede leather with a nice thick lining. It wasn't long before they were shivering.

"Now you understand what these people go through every day, living on the streets in these conditions," I said sternly. "You show up, give them hope and all you do is move them somewhere else for some silly reason. It is time to fess up, or more of your clothing will go to these needy folks. I doubt any of them care if you freeze or not."

I waited and they didn't talk. I had T gather up their jackets and hand them to the first two people he saw. They looked at them for a minute, studying the nice material and then grabbed them and ran yelling thank you, once I assured them it was theirs to keep.

"Do we now have you take off your boots?" I said, noticing some nice leather on each of their feet. "I'm sure we won't have an issue finding someone with the same shoe size who is in need of warmer footwear."

"Okay," bellowed the now very cold driver. "We work for Boss Builders."

"They're out of business. I need a better answer."

He hesitated and I started waving at their feet.

"Order came down from the new owners," explained the black man, his spirit breaking quickly in the frosty air. "Liquid

48

Investors."

"A person's name calling the shots?" I wanted it all.

"Not certain. A woman. Said she was part of the marketing team in town. I think it was Maxina or a name like that."

I smiled and pulled out my cellphone.

"We're going to get this on the record," I proclaimed. "Any objections and we'll have you barefooted on this frosty pavement. Is that understood?"

Both agreed and I began recording their confession, as light snow began to fall, adding to their misery. Once we were done, I made a call to the Denver police, and after a convincing conversation with the dispatch, they made it a priority and had several units there in a hurry.

Chapter 10

I was sitting in a moderately comfortable chair on the second floor of a modern three-story business complex down in Centennial. I was leafing through a sports magazine, passing the time waiting for a meeting with one of the local bigwigs with Liquid Investors.

I'd asked to speak with Maxina but was told that would be difficult to arrange as her schedule was quite full. This left me to meet with her assistant, Kyley Farrow, instead. Both were part of the marketing and publicity group for this local branch. I told them I had important information that might tarnish the company name I wanted to discuss. They were able to squeeze me in for a quick sit down six days before Christmas.

The magazine didn't hold my interest, so I thought about the events after the police arrived. Both men were questioned, but neither were in a talking mood after the black and white squad cars showed. Since each was armed, they were checked for permits, which both possessed. After thinking it over, there was little they could be charged with. Coercion and threats of violence might not hold up in court and certainly wouldn't lead to any real jail time. Kidnapping was a possibility but none of the homeless would speak up and I had obviously been baiting the two men.

If anything, they wanted to have *me* charged for holding a gun on them. But after discussing what I was doing, the officers laughed it off and let them drive away with only a warning, each now needing to buy a new coat and gloves, while being out the money they had given me and T, which we distributed to several of the homeless.

I had figured there wouldn't be much to hold them on when I had concocted the plan but didn't care. I had learned from the two men that Liquid Investors had ordered the homeless people removed from the building because they wanted to purchase it as part of a large block of real estate in the area they aspired to own and develop. It was a two-fold plan, for they desired to also purchase the Mission as well, since it was part of the same area of real estate they were gobbling up. No more homeless in the region, no more need for the shelter.

While I continued my interrogation, T had made the rounds and found several of the people who had been taken away, including Parker's close friend. Most wanted to go back to the old building, as all their worldly possessions were there. We arranged to get them transportation back via bus, with the help of the police. About twenty people in all were taken back to what they called home. There were others who had been moved from different locations within that same area. The police did their best to render them assistance, calling in some local resources who dealt with the homeless to lend a helping hand.

After getting this all squared away, a day later I checked on Parker and he was healing nicely and would be able to leave the hospital in the next day or so. He was pleased to hear what we had learned, thrilled we had found those that had been moved out, unharmed. I had arranged for him to stay at The Mission of the Invisible Souls, as Sam was happy to help him out, putting him up in one of the spare rooms. This would allow him time to heal and get back up on his feet again.

Today Barry was supposed to meet me at the Liquid Investors office, but he was running late. Fortunately, my 9 a.m. meeting was also running late by about thirty minutes. When Barry walked in, dressed in a sharp gray suit and wild tie of rainbow colors, we were ushered off to a small meeting room where Kyley was already sitting. She stood up shaking our hands and offering us coffee, juice, milk or water. Barry was a big coffee addict and wanted a cup. I decided on juice and we all sat down once our drinks were prepared and sitting in front of us.

Kyley was probably in her early thirties, dressed in a dark pant suit, with white heels which made her quite statuesque. She had long reddish-brown hair tied into a ponytail in back, and a pair of reading glasses hanging around her neck. She was all business when she first spoke, once she was finished typing on her notebook computer.

"Gentlemen, I'm sorry I made you wait. Busy day and I likely can only give you a few minutes to hear what you have to say. I believe, Mister Mann, you mentioned some *issue* you've discovered that could tarnish our company name."

I glanced at Barry, already perturbed they were trying to rush us through this. But there was no way we weren't going to take all the time we needed to hammer home our point.

"I did," I said. "I will try to come straight to the point. Employees of your company have been forcing homeless people out of where they live and in one case even attacked and stabbed one of them, injuring him severely."

"I highly doubt that to be the case," she said bluntly, not hesitating to disagree with my statement, a stern expression on her rouge cheeks.

"We have contrary evidence which says otherwise. The men were working for a company, Boss Builders, which you recently purchased."

"We own many companies. That hardly means we're involved with any of the doings of the employees."

I tried not to snicker. "Those employees have told us otherwise. Two of them, one of which stabbed the client of mine, also were recently found dead before they could be arraigned."

"Are you accusing our company of having been involved with their deaths?"

I had learned from the autopsy the deaths were drug induced. So far though there had been nothing to prove it was anything other than accidental.

"I have no proof of it. Both died from drug overdoses. The circumstances are fishy but can't be proven. In time, and with my persistence, that can change."

"Did these two men confess to working for us after attacking your client?" She appeared unmoved by my words.

"No. They died before speaking. But two others, who came in their place, did say as much. Claiming your boss, Maxina, called them to finish the work of the two who died. All of which I recorded for the record."

I pulled out my phone and played for her the confession. She put on her glasses and watched. After it was over, she didn't appear shocked by what she heard them say. She was privy to the plan, there was no doubt, despite her pleading ignorance.

"You have names of these two?"

I gave her both their names, which she typed into her computer.

"Both men were also armed at the time I confronted them." I added.

"Weapons I'm assuming they had a legal right to carry."

52

I nodded.

"And how did you come across these two men?"

"I was undercover as a homeless person. They approached me and several others offering us money and a job if we came with them. All they really were doing was relocating them to another part of the city, to get them off the property you wanted to purchase."

"You have an address of this building?"

I gave her the information.

"What is your profession, Mister Mann?" She wasn't looking at me, only staring down, typing away on her computer.

"I'm a private detective."

"Mister Anders, in what capacity are you here?"

"Lawyer to the man who was stabbed and the others who were falsely coerced into moving."

"And you plan to take legal action?"

"Only if necessary," stated Barry. "We were hoping to come to some type of an arrangement that allows all of us to get what we want."

She looked up from her computer screen. "I see. You plan to blackmail us."

Barry smirked at her statement. "Negotiation is a kinder word I'd use in this case."

"Who has seen the video?" Kyley asked while looking at me.

"Only the two of us. Of course, that can also change quickly. Posted on the internet, it can spread and be shared faster than lightning. Once that happens there is no stopping it."

Kyley rocked back in her chair, glasses hanging again, crossing her legs, her hands gripping the armrests, her eyes closed as if in deep thought. She took five minutes and then got up, excusing herself, promising to return. I prepared myself for the worst.

"What do you think?" I asked of Barry.

"Hard to say. Hopefully they will come to understand it's in their best interests to pay up."

"Or they could send security in here and toss us out," I quipped.

He smirked at me. "That's why you're here, to prevent that."

I smiled. *Yes, that was true.* I drank down the rest of my juice to bolster my strength in case it was needed. About ten minutes later she came back in, thankfully alone.

53

"I confirmed the two men did work for Boss Builders. I have talked with my manager. She says you need to state what you're wanting, and we'll weigh if it really is in our best interest. If it is, we'll get our lawyers involved and work out a settlement. But I warn you, trying to blackmail us into overpaying will lead to dire consequences. Is that understood?"

It sounded like a threat. But I had one of my own.

"It is. But understand us," I replied. "If you don't deal with us fairly, or try any type of intimidation or threats, all this information will go to the local news outlets and be spread across the internet, including the recordings of the confessions by the two men you witnessed and statements from several of the homeless who were coerced away. All this is put away safely and securely, ready to be released if necessary. Which we hope isn't the case, as no one wins and it doesn't help our clients as much as it would if you settled."

With a huff, she agreed. She pulled out a digital tape recorder, as did Barry. Both pressed play and each noted the parties had agreed to allow the recording.

"We want all of Parker Turner's medical bills covered," stated Barry. "He was the man who was stabbed by one of the Boss Builders' men. His care is still ongoing, so we don't know the amount yet, but it will be substantial. I'm sure you can negotiate with the hospital a fair settlement, once the bill is due."

Even with the recording Kyley was making notes on her computer, her glasses sitting on her nose again.

"Second, the people living in the building will be paid a relocation fee of one thousand dollars each. This will allow them to move gracefully to a new location, and possibly get their life in order. If they have skills, you can also help them find new employment if they want it. Or offer to pay for job training."

"You realize we can legally force these people out," Kyley declared.

Barry leaned forward in his seat, glaring at her. "You can, but if that was the case, you would have already. You didn't want to look like heartless corporate monsters throwing homeless out into the cold. You were trying to be sneaky and do it under the radar but got caught. This way you can look like good Samaritans helping them find a better place to live."

She nodded her head. "Go on."

"Thirdly, you need to leave the Mission of the Invisible Souls alone. Allow them to continue to help the homeless in the area and run their shelter. If you're concerned the building doesn't live up to the levels of the new complex of structures you want to create, then help them raise funds to upgrade their facility so it meets your standards. You can even donate some additional land adjacent to their building to create a buffer. You can do this any way you feel works best for your corporation. No matter what you do it will make you look like white knights helping those who are unfortunate. Think of the positive PR it will create."

Barry's summation had been perfect, covering exactly as we discussed. He⸱ was in his element, a master at litigation and it showed, by the joy on his face.

"Is that all?" asked Kyley, with a hint of sarcasm.

"Use your political power to help those who fought for their country to get the assistance they need and deserve," I added. "Several of these people put their lives on the line and suffer from injuries, both physical and mental, that the VA now seems unprepared to help them with. As a powerful corporation, you have avenues to the decision makers that we can't access. The ability to twist arms to get things moving for them. I'm sure Tyrell Powers has a few congressmen and senators in his back pocket he can manipulate."

Her eyes moved to meet mine when she heard the name. I wasn't sure if it was fear, or surprise I'd said it. Either way, she knew, we knew who the major player in her company was.

"We want to work with you to find a happy solution for all, so this doesn't get messy," noted Barry. "Believe us when we say that we're prepared and willing to go that route if necessary."

"And what of your persistence in investigating the two deaths?" stated Kyley.

"So long as you agree to our terms," I replied. "Then there is no need for me to stick my nose where it doesn't belong."

"And if we don't?"

Shifting forward in my seat, I spoke with clear confidence. "Then I have a tendency to be a real pain in the ass!"

Kyley leaned back in her chair, glancing over her digital notes, pondering what to do. We had placed our demands, for them to decide. Neither Barry or I thought it was too much to ask, though

55

they might think otherwise. She agreed to get with her superiors and get back to us. We made it clear we wanted a quick answer, or else for the holidays they would be made to look like Scrooge.

We wrapped things up, Barry grabbing his digital recorder for safe keeping and headed down to the main entrance.

As we checked out with security, there was a black man standing in the doorway. He was dressed in nice tailored black suit, with polished black boots. His hands covered with leather fingerless gloves, the right hand holding expensive sunglasses, the bulge of a large gun barely concealed under his jacket. His eyes glistened; a stare to freeze and scare. Diamond stud earrings glinted in each lobe, a dark, neatly trimmed goatee framed his chin and his dark brown head was shaved to a fine stubble of coarse black hair.

As I walked past, I met his cold gaze of intimidation with a joyful smile, as I mouthed the words "Merry Christmas, Wolfe" while pointing at him. I felt his eyes follow me all the way to my car, knowing it wouldn't be the last time I'd see him. A new dangerous foe I'd someday have to come up against. A future moment in time I wasn't looking forward to.

Chapter 11

My day started off with a morning jog through my neighborhood, braving the December chill, four days before Christmas. I was feeling loose and confident about what I'd accomplished, happy to lend a hand with the homeless situation but knowing there were many more out there needing assistance.

My pace was steady as I'd covered the entire alleyway that ran on the backside of my home. It didn't take long to reach East Warren Ave, cutting to my left, careful of any icy pavement and then down South Sherman, when I heard a vehicle coming up fast behind me, pulling on past before spinning sideways to cut me off.

The large champagne colored Chevy SUV squealed, the brakes and tires testing their limits. Once stopped, the smell of burnt rubber and ceramics clogging the air, out jumped two enormous white men, both in expensive black suits exhibiting large handguns held at their side.

"Jarvis Mann, you need to come with us," demanded the first man, large enough to block the sun.

I wasn't armed, figuring my jog didn't require firepower, so I wasn't in much of a position to argue. It was in my nature to resist and be as difficult as possible, but my slim odds against a bullet weren't worth testing.

"Where are you taking me?" I inquired, even though I doubted they would tell me.

"You'll find out soon enough," he replied. "No harm will come to you, if you don't resist."

I wasn't sure if I believed him, especially with the weapons they were displaying.

"And if I do?"

He held the gun up to his chest, as a warning, no words needed.

I nodded, getting into the backseat, sliding over to allow the man who had spoken to sit next to me. The second man joined another in the front, the driver only slightly smaller, soon taking us to who knows where. I felt like a tiny sardine in a can of huge tunas.

"Do you guys get your steroids at a bulk discount?" I blurted out, even though it probably wasn't a good idea.

The man next to me grunted. "Shut up!"

"Or maybe too much gamma radiation?"

"If you don't keep your mouth shut, I will smash you!"

I grinned, figuring he'd answered my question with his response, and it would be best I not make him mad and confirm it.

The SUV was soon out of my neighborhood, travelling down Broadway. After several blocks we pulled into a lot which used to be a car dealership, now closed, the space devoid of any cars. In the center of the lot was a square shaped beige stucco building, with a rimmed royal blue painted overhang and pitched roof. A dirty outline was all that remained of where the dealership sign once proudly shone.

Getting out of the SUV, I was led up the stained wooden steps to an attached deck and then inside, the brown carpeted space open and empty, other than two tables. One smaller one against the wall had refreshments and food; donuts, bagels, coffee, juice and water. A larger table was stationed in the center of the room, with several cushioned, ash-colored chairs circling it, a huge digital screen, probably 100 inches in size, mounted to the beige wall, the table positioned for easy viewing.

At the head of the table sat a black man in a gunmetal-gray suit, wearing an ebony fur coat, which probably cost the lives of too many cute creatures to count. He stood up, showing his height to be about 6'1" with a solid build of a man who worked out. Walking over, he displayed a golden smile—literally—since he had two gold teeth, a tight, short afro with specs of gray and the steely brown eyes of a confident, wealthy man, who I remembered from the picture I saw on the internet.

"This would be the mighty, Jarvis Mann," he stated confidently.

He circled me, gazing up and down, appearing to size me up, not impressed with me or my jogging clothes from the expression on his clean-shaven face. Done with his stroll, he stood before me.

"Though you've lived in Denver many years, you aren't a native, having been born in Des Moines, Iowa. Moved out here in your twenties, where you worked security, then worked for a detective agency, that you didn't care for, since you didn't like those in authority telling you what to do. With the help of your father, who gave you a sizeable amount of cash, you started your own private eye business, mostly living day to day until you hooked up with Brandon Sparks and got your ten minutes of fame which you parlayed into a relatively successful business."

It would seem he had done his homework and knew much about me. Not that any of it was hard to discover if you dug deep enough.

"And you would be Tyrell Powers," I answered back with the same zest. "Founder and CEO of Powers USA Inc with offices in many cities around the country, including Denver. Looking spry for forty-eight, with several business degrees from Yale, you made your name in construction but have expanded into other areas, mostly via Liquid Investors. A man who will aggressively go after what he wants, and even work the market to lower the price by whatever means necessary."

"I'm honored you know me," Tyrell declared with great pride.

"I wish I could say the same," I responded with a hint of spite.

"Such a confident statement to make from a man brought to me so easily."

I shrugged. "If I'd been armed, it might have been a different story. But the shoulder holster ruins the outline of my sweats. Hard for me to say no to the armed twin towers here without firepower. Do you feed them Miracle-Gro?"

Powers smiled. "*There* is the humor I've heard tales of. I think you'll find there is nothing funny about the situation you're in."

"Probably not, but it won't stop me from trying out my material on you before open mic night. But let's stop pussy footing around and get to why you forcefully brought me here." I upped my spite meter.

He ignored my humor and anger, instead clapping his hands twice. "You look hungry. Let's get you something to eat."

From the other room strolled in a tall, slender man, in white long-sleeved dress shirt; bowtie, vest, slacks and highly polished shoes, all in black.

"Can you get Mister Mann something to eat, Jeeves?" announced Tyrell.

"Yes sir. What would you like?" He looked at me with no emotion.

"I'll take orange juice and a maple frosted donut."

He nodded and walked over to the other table. I looked at Tyrell, shaking my head.

"Jeeves?" I said in surprise.

59

"I know. I found it funny myself when he applied for the job. Hearing the name screams manservant. I've never asked if it's his real name or not. But how can you refuse to hire someone as a servant who's using that moniker?"

Jeeves carried over the drink and donut on a small plastic plate, sitting it on the table before me.

"Will that be all, sir?" he said, standing at attention.

"You may leave," answered Tyrell. "I will call if we need anything else."

"Very well, sir," he responded before leaving the room.

Tyrell moved to sit in the chair he occupied when I first walked in. "Please have a seat, Jarvis, for I want to show you what we have planned."

He pointed at the chair next to where he sat, so I grabbed the cushiony back and settled in, contemplating what he had in store for me.

"Since you appear to know so much about me, I'm wondering if you know what I'm doing here in Denver."

"Acquisitions, from what I've heard," I replied, before taking a bite of the donut, the fresh and warm taste as if it recently came out of the fryer.

"Correct. A whole section here along Broadway I've bought, or will be buying, to revitalize this area."

"Building retail, office space and condos for rent or to sell." I took a drink of the orange juice. It was likely fresh squeezed for it was excellent.

"Exactly. A big boom for the local economy." Tyrell beamed with glee.

I frowned. "Sold at an exorbitant price which will push out and displace many people because the cost is too high for them to live here. The only boom will be for the fat cats like yourself, making a killing at the expense of others."

Tyrell frowned. "The circle of life in the business world."

"Cute," I commented. "Yet you tried to relocate the homeless people out of the area via bribes or intimidation, with some success, until your boys stabbed one them."

Tyrell leaned back in his chair crossing his arms, unmoved by the accusation.

"They weren't working on behalf of orders given by me or my

company. If I recall correctly, those men are dead now, thanks to an overdose of drugs. Probably hyped up when they attacked that poor man."

Though he sounded truthful, I wasn't buying it.

"Yet, after their demise, two other men were sent to start the harassment again. I was undercover when they arrived offering money to leave with them. When they tried to drop me and another man off downtown, we confronted them. They then gave me a full statement, which I recorded, pointing the blame at Liquid Investors. A company you have a major stake in."

Tyrell appeared unconvinced, waving off my words. "Weak evidence at best."

"Then you attempted to buy The Mission of the Invisible Souls through your law firm, Krieg & Williamson. Fortunately, the church is not in the business of making a profit, like you are, and refused to sell, even after you upped your offer. Those men who were arrested tried to intimidate Pastor Sam, but she kicked their butt. How did it feel to have your men bested by woman?"

Tyrell didn't answer but picked up the remote for the TV and turned it on. On the screen was a mockup drawing of how the new location will look when it was finished. I was not sure why he was showing me this. Maybe he was bragging about what he was about to accomplish, hoping to impress me. But it didn't work, as I raised my hands in a shrug to say 'so what.'

"There is a *lot* of cash to be made with this project," Tyrell stated. "Though, along with your lawyer buddy and your aggressive negotiation play at Liquid Investors, there will be less now. Which doesn't please me any. I could offer you a bribe, but it would appear money for you isn't your endgame, is it?"

"Per the deal we offered, money for the homeless and money for the Mission," I replied. "A small price for you to pay to keep this out of the news. I'm sure the politicians who will be involved in rezoning all this land for your project, would be inclined to deny those requests, if word got out. You'll make a few dollars less on the entire endeavor. Though I doubt you'll have to start purchasing your wardrobe from Walmart because of it."

Tyrell leaned forward, with a stern expression. "You're right, I won't end up in the poor house. And on advice from counsel, we'll make the deal and settle this quietly. But I don't like the idea of some flatfoot private eye blackmailing me. It sends the wrong message I don't want people to get wind of—one leaving me looking weak and vulnerable."

I blotted a napkin to my face, having finished my donut and juice.

"If you make right by these poor souls, I won't ever say a word. And your reputation won't be ruined." I stood up from the chair, sensing this might be leading to aggressive action I may not care for. "I think it's time for me to leave, for your attempts to intimidate me aren't going to work."

As I turned to walk out, I heard fingers snapping, the first large man moving over to block me. He had short blonde hair, a broad face with razor burn, and a nose that appeared to have been broken a time or two. Slugging this rock of a man in the stomach or jaw, would likely lead to a bruised or broken hand, with little effect on him. Kicking him in the testicles was an option, but his massive thighs created a natural wall in front of his groin. Still everyone had a weak spot to attack which I had summed up when I first saw him.

He stood before me with stern expression, hands on his side, jacket open, showing his holstered gun. I shrugged my shoulders, then slowly put my gloved hands up while moving forward, and then with my quick reflexes, drove the palm of my hand up into his throat, the force causing him to gasp for air, as he clutched his thick neck, staggering backward in pain.

I sensed the second man coming at me from behind, his gun drawn, and I used the first man as a shield, getting behind him, and then forcefully pushing him into the other man. As he shrugged off the body as it struck him, I stepped around and, with full force, kicked with the bottom of my foot into the right knee, the audible crack nearly as loud as his scream, as the second man buckled down, hitting the floor in agony.

With both men disabled, I looked around to see if there was anyone else to challenge me, but only saw Tyrell standing, seething anger in his eyes, pointing a shiny silver-plated 9mm gun at me. I glared him square in the eye with a force of determination to match his anger.

"You should have brought Wolfe with you today," I declared over the injured moans of his men. "It would seem the B-team wasn't good enough."

"A mistake I'll not make again," he replied, the gun barrel like an evil eye steadily pointed at me.

I turned away, moving towards the door, not caring to stick around and debate.

"Stop or I'll shoot," Tyrell announced.

"If you want to shoot me in the back, go ahead," I said, while walking, never looking behind me. "But I plan on strolling out of here, finishing my jog and stopping by The Mission of the Invisible Souls to see what type of help I can provide them. I suggest you put away your over polished gun and figure out the best way you can help them to get a little positive press, before this whole mess blows up in your face. For killing me won't stop the world from knowing what a slime ball you are."

I made it out the door, heart racing, but no bullet forthcoming, and hit the street jogging feeling even cockier than I did earlier, which probably wasn't the right mood to be in for I'd made a powerful man angry. But at this moment I really didn't give a damn!

Chapter 12

It was Christmas day and I was standing, serving food at The Mission of the Invisible Souls. On each side of me was April and Bill, who had both volunteered. Bill's family; wife, son and daughter, were also there helping the throng of people from the streets looking for a hot meal and time with others on this joyous holiday.

I couldn't believe how many wandered in, looking for dinner to fill their normally empty stomachs. There was plenty of food; turkey, ham, potatoes, rolls, stuffing and cranberry sauce. For dessert, various pies, like pumpkin, apple and cherry, their fresh baked smells filling the air. Much of it had been donated from those happy to help. It was great to see the outpouring of support, but sad to witness so many still in need. And not just for today, but for many days before and after.

I did my part, but it never felt like enough. I had helped those who had been living in the abandoned building get shelter here at the Mission, and a deal was in the works with Liquid Investors to get them some working money, the goal of getting them back on their feet. The large corporation was hesitant to assist, evident by my confrontation with Tyrell Powers. But Barry and I would continue to turn the screws and, in the end, they would have no choice other than to agree to our terms, though they might drag their feet in promptly paying up.

Barry even lent some time to assist today, though he flatly refused to do dishes, not wanting to ruin his perfectly manicured nails. Even with his generosity of lowering his percent taken for any settlement, I wondered if he would add it to a future bill of mine for his services. Pro bono was not a term he used often, for he preferred getting paid full price for his services, which showed in the clothes he wore and the car he drove.

Both Parker and T were at the Mission today, as we had found them some assistance through the VA's Homeless Veteran's program that Barry had discovered perusing the endless sea of government web pages. A program to help them with housing and health care, both physical and mental, something many sorely needed. Assistance lost in the bureaucratic shuffle most homeless veterans never knew existed. The paperwork had been filed, now it was a matter of how long it would take to make its way through the endless government red tape. Sam offered them jobs at the Mission in the meantime, with a small stipend to help them get back into a more normal life, if that was even possible.

As for Liquid Investors and Powers USA, they would soon be in control of most of the real estate in the area, with plans to begin a huge rebuild of a large section of Broadway that spanned many blocks. But they had pledged with our encouragement, at least verbally so far, to leave the Mission alone and even support it. They were a mega corporation who would make tens of millions on the new buildings in sales and leasing once it was all completed.

It would be a boost for the area, creating new jobs and influx of cash once it was all done in several years. But would it benefit the poor or only the rich, as the housing costs would likely be out of reach for many, possibly forcing more to the streets, with affordable housing being a common cause of homelessness. Time would tell, but at least for The Mission of the Invisible Souls, the value of their building would increase, as would the need. And with donations, upgrades would be in the works to better serve everyone using their services.

After the lines subsided, I myself grabbed a helping of food, the overwhelming smells playing with my senses, and found a seat, sitting next to Parker, his best friend and T.

"Thank you for all you've done," said Parker, clean shaven and hardly recognizable for the first time since we'd met, but still moving slowly from his healing injury. "There is hope for many of us now. In time, we may have a chance to find our way."

I searched the room around me, seeing men, women and children of all races, trying to get by, somehow finding a way to survive the mean streets. Tattered clothing, worn out boots, dirty faces, many showing joy, which was a rarity. Savoring a filling meal most of us took for granted each day. Plentiful food they might be lucky enough to get a couple times a month. I had done what I could, but it wasn't enough, as there were more in need with each passing day. Transparent to many, like they had been to me.

"Thank you for helping me see what I never saw before," I replied. "All of these invisible souls are now visible. Maybe we can get more people to see you as more than someone standing on a street corner holding a sign."

We can only hope!

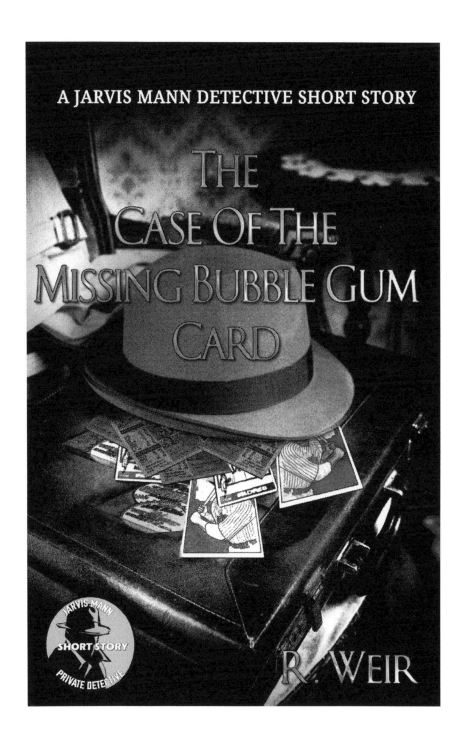

A JARVIS MANN DETECTIVE SHORT STORY

THE CASE OF THE MISSING BUBBLE GUM CARD

R. WEIR

Now as a special bonus,
for the first time in print:
The initial
Jarvis Mann Detective Mystery

The Case of the Missing Bubble Gum Card

A Jarvis Mann Detective Short Story

By

R Weir

Copyediting by:
YM Zachery and JB Joseph Editing Services

Cover Design by:
Happi Anarky
www.happianarky.com

The Case...

I drove westward on Evans Street enjoying the beauty of the day, the driver's door window cracked slightly open on my 1969 Mustang Boss 302. The afternoon sun filled the western sky and warmed me through the marred windshield.

Despite what most people outside of Denver think, winter isn't always freezing cold with snow up to your waist. On the contrary, this February day gave us sun with temperatures nearing 60 degrees. A light wind in the crisp air stirred the city's fresh, though at times tainted, aura. I missed my turn while admiring the fanny of a lovely woman walking down the street. It had been worth the extra drive, for it really was one glorious spandex concealed behind.

Making a left turn onto Broadway once the light had changed, I turned left again a block later down Warren past Lincoln and left into the alleyway. Dodging trash dumpsters, I drove cautiously down the already narrow backstreet. Pulling into my parking space on a small, deserted paved lot which faced Evans, I shut off the heavily travelled engine.

The building I lived in was a raised dual level built after World War Two. I'd rented the lower half for several years now, calling it home. The bland gray color, with brown wood slats surrounding the outer middle third of the building's main body, didn't add much ambiance to the area. The neighborhood stood reasonably quiet, while at times adventurous. Walking the streets at night wasn't advised, and never should be done alone, though one might say that about most neighborhoods these days. The area had a good mix of cultures, with all races represented. No cushy suburb for me—but a real city with real city people and problems, the kind of environment I'd always wanted to live and work in.

My home served as a place of business too. A cheap plastic white placard with deep blue lettering anchored to the brick wall read *"MANN PRIVATE INVESTIGATOR."* The mere words made one tremble with fear, though the sign itself was a letdown. One day I hoped to have a large, luminous one, with lots of flashing lights. The more colors the better. Unfortunately, the low balance bank account dictates for now, squashing those dreams of seeing my name in neon.

In thirty-five plus years of life, I've been doing P.I. work for the last ten, seven of which in my own practice. The glamour of the job had worn off after the first domestic case. The woman who had hired me took the shocking news about her husband's infidelity out on me with the coffee cup she held in her hand. The scalding hot liquid had certainly burned the skin, while the stain from the horrid mud ruined my favorite gray sport coat, tarnishing my attempted G.Q. image. Her itemized bill not only included the cost of the jacket, but the shattered cup as well.

Getting out of the Mustang, I noticed him; the young lad sitting at the top of the stairwell. To describe him as a boy would have been unfair, though he wasn't quite a man either. He appeared to be fifteen, possibly sixteen years old.

As I approached, he rose to his feet, my detective eyes deducing that he stood about 5'7", with around 150 pounds of solid athletic build. Dressed in faded blue jeans, LeBron James T-shirt and sneakers, the young African-American gave a cautious smile. He appeared to be a bit nervous.

"Good afternoon," I said cordially. "Waiting for someone?"

"Do you work here?" he asked with hesitation.

"Do you need a trim?" I proclaimed, referring to my upstairs neighbor, the hair designer business which was closed on Sunday and Monday.

"No," he stated while pointing at the sign.

"Beautiful, wouldn't you say?" I remarked. "Draws in the clients from miles around!" I wasn't trying to be snarky—just my usual off-the-cuff banter.

"Are you a private detective?" he stated with no conviction in his voice.

I found it difficult to believe he couldn't tell. My current appearance apparently didn't present itself as tough enough for the line of work. Most people think we wear leather from head to toe—fedora, jacket, pants and boots. I wore an old brown leather jacket on my fit torso, which was all the cowhide I could afford besides my tennis shoes. Black denim jeans and a gray sweatshirt didn't ideally give me that macho tough guy look. With my sarcastic sense of humor, he probably thought I did standup comedy, which is a common mistake many folks made.

"When there's private detective work to do," I replied proudly.

"You look different than the actors on television." More disdain in his tone.

"Just don't tell my mother. She wanted me to be a doctor. I wore a stethoscope around my neck when she used to come to visit." Not even a smile crossed his face. The humor seemed lost on him.

"I hoped you'd be available to hire as I have a lost possession, I need your help locating."

I looked him over carefully. He seemed like a polite and sincere person. I was currently in between cases, which is normal if the truth be known. It wouldn't hurt to hear what he had to say. The possibility of making money always got my attention.

"Come inside. You look cold without a jacket. It's warm out, but not that warm."

Down the steps to the lower half of the building took us to where I lived and conducted my business. The big-time detective agencies have large fancy buildings, with lobbies, elevators, and secretaries. My lobby was an outdated kitchen, though it was for the most part clean. I had a secretary for about two weeks once, an old girlfriend who helped me out. Unfortunately, she found out I'd slept with another woman and quit on me in a fit of fiery anger. For some reason she never used me as a reference.

Today my only secretary turned out to be a fifty-dollar digital answering machine. It was always on time, polite to the customers, and couldn't care less if you didn't feel like talking after intimacy. Though the black box certainly wouldn't look or smell as lovely and it was hardly enticing to curl up with at night.

The little red light wasn't flashing, which meant no one wanted my services. The LED would last forever, for it rarely blinked. Apparently, the snappy greeting scared people off before they spoke. A masterfully designed website would be cool, while my Yellow Pages advertisement should be larger than one line, but cost remained an obstacle.

I could have politely turned the lad down, but with nothing of importance going on today, I'd hear him out and see if he'd surprise me with the case of the century.

"I'm Jarvis Mann," I proclaimed. "Have a seat."

He sat in one of the stiff wood chairs reserved for clients. No fancy furniture in my living room, which also served as my office.

Just an old desk and two chairs, both made of pine, a pair of white metal four drawer filing cabinets and a worn brown sofa and matching recliner. Papers covered the top of the desk, neatly piled for easy reference, an LCD Monitor and keyboard to one side attached to a desktop computer sitting underneath on the floor. Behind my desk I sat in a chair I'd slept in on many occasions. The cushy high back chocolate brown leather rocked and swiveled with the best of them. The fancy agencies had this type of quality furniture for all to sit in. But my rates were better.

"I feel strange asking you for help," the lad confessed, his eyes focused on the polished natural wood floor.

I tried to put him at ease. "Why don't you tell me your name first?"

"Dennis Gash," he answered, his eyes now staring my way.

After hearing the name, I had to ask. "Do you play football, Dennis?"

"I'm a running back in high school," he answered with surprise in his voice. "How did you know?"

"A wild guess." With a name like Gash, one had to play football. John Madden would love this guy. A touch of mud, blood, and sweat gripping his clothing would be the clincher.

"I'm a sophomore so I didn't play much this year. Coach says if I continue to grow, I might be a starter in the future. I'm extremely fast but need to get stronger. With a little work I hope to be like my favorite running back, Adrian Peterson."

Adrian Peterson was a future NFL Hall of Famer. A running back that came along once in a generation, like Jim Brown. Dennis was compact in size, making it challenging for him to reach that stature. But smaller backs can be great too, like my personal favorite, the now retired Barry Sanders. Sometimes heart is more important than size.

"Dennis, what can I help you with?" A question the expensive agencies would ask. *Where did these brainwaves come from!*

"A valuable item of mine was stolen and I'd like you to help me find it."

"Tell me?" More snappy questions. I had a million of them.

He looked apprehensive. "You're going to laugh, but it's valuable to me. Someone stole a baseball card of mine."

Holding back the laughter, I'd hear him out. *No, not the case of the century.*

"I can tell you're not interested," said Dennis, sounding disheartened. "I should go." He started to rise but I waved for him to sit.

"I must say that it's not every day someone comes in and asks me to find a bubble gum card."

He looked put off by my words. "Not just any old bubble gum card. This one is worth quite a bit of money—almost twelve hundred and fifty dollars. If my dad found out, he'd kill me."

From the sincere look on the lad's face and the way he was squirming in the chair, one would only guess the punishment he'd have in store. Still I wasn't convinced I could lend assistance.

"Dennis, are you sure you didn't lose or misplace it somewhere?" I asked, while leaning forward in my chair.

"I had the card yesterday morning, after carrying it to church in my coat pocket to show my friends. We placed it in penny sleeves and a top loader for protection, with a small sticker on the back bearing my name and address. Later we played around outside while our parents talked inside. I'd forgotten all about the card until I returned home. That's when I realized it was missing." He shook his head as if he was displeased with his mistake.

"Maybe it fell out of your pocket and is sitting in the back seat of your car. Did you drive to church?" I rested my elbows on the desktop, something my mother would have scolded me about doing.

"No, we always walk since it's close to home."

"It fell out somewhere between home and church," I concluded. "Someone would likely find and keep the card. I'd say chances of locating it are slim. Did you check with the church to see if someone turned it in?"

He nodded. "I did right away, and they didn't have it. That's when I remembered passing your house and noticing your sign. I thought...maybe..."

Wow, the plain banner worked. Time to save money and get rid of the wimpy Yellow Pages advertisement.

"Your parents' homeowner's insurance would probably cover the loss," I offered as a resolution.

"No. I *can't* tell my parents." His eyes scanned downward. "Father would be angry, and I don't want to disappoint him. He

74

gave me the card when I was about seven. Said he trusted me to take care of it, like his dad trusted him. If I continue to hold onto it, in time it would be worth a great deal of money."

Twelve hundred and fifty dollars was a significant amount of money to someone his age. *Hell, that was a lot of dinero to me!* Plus there was the sentimental value of a family heirloom passed down through the generations, which was now lost. I doubted the chances of finding the card. Still I put my P.I. mind to work, grasping for a brainstorm. In seconds, I came up with the most crucial question of the day.

"How much money do you have?" I asked, not expecting a big payday.

"I have about seventy-five dollars in a savings account," he replied, his eyes meeting mine.

"Do you realize what I charge per hour?" Lately that had been a big, fat, zero.

"No."

I told him my rate, his audible gasp filling the room.

"I could work a couple of days and eat up the value of that card, plus your savings account and not be successful in tracking it down."

"I have other cards that have value, though not as much as this one." His eyes filled with anguish. "Please help me!"

The magic word broke down my resistance. I wasn't sure there was anything to do to help, but I had nothing planned this afternoon and no good sports games were on TV. Time to negotiate a deal.

"Sometimes I do jobs for insurance companies for a finder's fee. Usually it pays between ten and twenty percent of the value of the merchandise. Here's what I'll do. I go around with you this afternoon and ask about the card. You can pay me in value with another card from your collection if it turns up. Adding up to ten to twenty percent of the lost card's value. If we don't find it, then you owe me nothing. But you must tell your father you lost it."

"But he'll be mad at me!" he proclaimed with concern.

"I'll go in and help you explain. That's the deal. Take it or leave it." Pausing for his reaction, I saw the realization on his face. "I'd say that's fair, wouldn't you?"

Dennis nodded his head. This was his only hope. I didn't figure we'd find the card, but at least he would own up to his father like a man, which is never easy for someone his age. I remembered that horrible feeling of admitting fault to my dad, and the anticipation of the oncoming punishment and the fear I felt. And growing up, fault had been a big part my life.

"What card did you lose?" More high-tech questions.

"A Topps Ernie Banks rookie card."

Any true baseball fan knew the name. He was Mr. Cub and a legend in the Chicago area, with a statue of him outside Wrigley Field.

"You're a Chicago Cubs fan, I gather."

"Yea. My dad and his dad too," stated Dennis proudly. "Grandpa got the card in 1954. He bought others as well, but Ernie was his favorite. Even after he'd given, thrown away, or lost many others in his collection, he'd cherished Ernie the most. He found out how much the card was worth and protected it from deteriorating. Condition of the card is where its main value is judged and this one is near mint. Its value increases every year I keep the card. Grandpa told me he paid about ten cents for the whole pack. A massive increase in market price if you ask me."

I whistled. "I'll say. I wish the stock in my business had appreciated that much through the years. The certificates are only good for placemats right now."

More wit lost on Dennis. Little did he know my jokes would someday be worth more than the Ernie Banks card. Good thing my humor was currently free of charge.

"Okay let's get started," I said, rising from my chair. "We'll follow the path you took to church and talk to your friends who joined you that day. Maybe they can shed light on what may have happened."

"Are you going to carry a gun with you?" asked Dennis, now standing.

The stigma of television. I suppose TV Private Eye's wore their guns in the shower.

"Do you think we'll need a gun?" I asked with a smirk.

"I'm not sure."

"Maybe if I flash a .38 at your friends they'll talk—tell us what we need to know."

His face blazed with a stunned expression. "We don't need to

76

do that!"

"I agree. I only carry a gun when absolutely necessary. And I don't care to even then. Let's see if we can solve this caper with our wits and if that doesn't work we'll come back for the heavy hardware."

Dennis broke out into a smile. I'd won him over. Next thing you know I'll have him laughing hysterically. Usually they didn't get hysterical until they received my bill.

I led the way outside to my old yellow and black striped car. He may have walked to church, but we were going to drive there this time. My six-foot, 180-pound frame was in decent shape, but the cool air of late afternoon began rolling in, and Dennis certainly wouldn't be able to stay up with my lightning pace. Besides I liked to do my part and add to the brown cloud that seemed to linger overhead during the winter months.

The inside of my Mustang made the outside seem like a jewel. The black vinyl seats were torn, the black vinyl dash cracked, the floor covered with trash and dirt. The AM/FM mono radio probably had tubes instead of transistors. The mileage on the speedometer had turned over several times, with somewhere around 387,000 miles on an engine which ran loud but smooth.

In seven years of driving I'd totaled about 95,000 miles of my own. I planned on making improvements as soon as the money started rolling in. New leather seats, a stereo with handsfree Bluetooth, and new speakers came first. This wasn't a shiny brand new BMW, but at least no one wanted to steal the relic in its current condition.

Dennis didn't appear to be overly impressed with my wheels. The passenger door creaked badly when he opened it. He sat down gingerly and looked down at the floorboard before he placed his feet. He slid the wrappers on the floor aside, the golden arches on them quite prevalent. Only the best in gourmet fast food for this P.I. A good portion of my meal time was spent in the drive-thru.

"I had to let the cleaning lady go the other day," I joked while starting the engine. "The cook as well!"

Backing the Mustang out into the alley, we pulled onto Evans. With Dennis directing, we turned almost immediately onto Sherman, then two blocks later east on Iliff until we came to his burnt umber brick home on Grant Street.

"This is where I live. We walked from here up a block to Our Lady of Lourdes Catholic Church." Dennis pointed forward, the Mustang taking less than a minute to arrive.

The church was a long narrow building made of soft brown brick, with stained glass windows gracing the south side. A very tall brick and stone outdoor temple with a statue of Jesus Christ erected out front. On the far north section of the block stood the church school and a house. In the middle of the property, a playground was built, and the leafless bushes and dead ivy looped along the chain linked fence. The playground combined grass, concrete and sand, with a wooden jungle gym and slide, basketball hoops, four square and hopscotch markings on the asphalt, and a rack for locking up bicycles.

A quick search of the grass and sand revealed no Ernie Banks card, though we did find a quarter and several wads of spent chewing gum. This did not satisfy my client. Time for the second phase of the job.

"Like you said, the card isn't here," I stated. "Do you know where the kids you played with live?"

"Yes. Three of them are close by."

"Okay, let's go talk with them and see if they can tell us something."

The first home sat across the street from the Harvard Recreation Center. Alonzo lived in a simple one-story tan brick structure, with layered white wood siding around the middle of the frame, badly in need of repainting. The roof was v-shaped, with steep slopes down both sides. A couple of leafless bushes and one tall evergreen graced the poorly kept front yard in need of seeding or sod. Parked in the driveway was an aqua mid-nineties Chevy pickup, which appeared to be in good shape except for the bed which was rusting through in spots.

Reaching the steps, I tried to ring the doorbell only to have Dennis inform me it didn't work. A vigorous knocking on the storm door got a response.

"Hey Dennis, how are you doing?" stated Alonzo with a smile.

"Not too bad. Can you come out for a minute, we need to talk."

"Sure."

Hollering to someone inside, he stepped outside, closing the door rather clumsily. He appeared to be of Spanish heritage, with very rich black curly hair and brown skin tone. His blue jeans were faded; his dull white jersey had dark lettering on the front spelling out 'Lincoln' which I cleverly deduced to be his high school. His canvas Nike sneakers were worn and in need of replacing. His simple dark windbreaker finished up his fashionable ensemble. He acted leery of me, never once glancing my way until introduced. With a polite handshake and short eye contact he turned back to his friend.

"What's up?" He had his hands in his jacket pocket for it was cooling off quickly.

"You remember yesterday at church I showed you the Ernie Banks card?" inquired Dennis.

"Sure. What about it?" He appeared unmoved by the question.

"When I got home it was missing. I was wondering if you might have seen it."

Alonzo turned and stared off into the distance, a look of distain on his face. "What's this guy got to do with it? Is he a cop or something?"

Apparently, C-O-P was traced all over my face. That strong authority figure in me always shined through.

"Sort of," replied Dennis, staring my way, not certain what else to say.

"Your friend here hired me to help him find his card. I'm a private detective." I pulled out my wallet and showed him the license which he glanced at.

Alonzo didn't know what to do, as my occupation made him nervous.

"Are you saying I took the card?" Anger began to show on his face.

"No man, I'm not," declared Dennis. "I'm wondering if you might have seen or heard about it disappearing. I just want the card back."

"Do you know how much the card is worth?" I asserted, adding my two cents. The question got Alonzo's ire up even more.

"What are you *implying*?" His voice seemed to hang on the last word.

"It's valuable to your friend here. And money sometimes clouds a person's judgment."

"I took it, is that what you're saying?" Alonzo's tone was just short of shouting.

"No. But I haven't heard you say you didn't." I gazed at him, gauging his reaction.

"Well I didn't. Ok. I don't steal from friends. At least those I thought to be my friend." Alonzo turned away again, his feelings hurt.

"Good enough," I said while turning and heading towards my car, convinced he was telling the truth.

As I got there I saw the two of them talking. The anger had receded, and they shook hands with a series of grips too complicated to explain. Even with months of practice I doubted I could duplicate it. The two separated, looking satisfied with the result.

Now with both of us back in the car, I wondered where to next.

"Why did you come down on him?" asked Dennis, a tinge of anger lacing his voice.

I turned my body to look at him. "Well sometimes you confront someone bluntly to get an honest answer. When you work in the world I do, it's easy for people to lie. Most everyone I encounter have an adversity to the truth. They live lies, becoming second nature to them. The direct approach sometimes is the best one. I came out and said what had to be said, pushing your friend to give me an answer."

"You believed him?" Dennis wondered, his eyebrows raised.

I nodded. "Yea, pretty much. I couldn't tell if he was avoiding me because of shyness, he hated authority figures, or I'm white."

"Maybe a little of all three. He's had problems with cops, his parents, and even a couple of white kids at school who are racist. His first response is to be cautious since you represent what he sees as the establishment."

I nodded, impressed by the words I'd heard. "Good analogy. How old are you?"

"I'll be sixteen in a month."

"You act older than your age. Tell me something, did *you* believe him?"

"Yea I did. He was being straight with me."

"I agree. Where to next?"

At the next stop we came up empty. The mother of his friend told us he went with his father to see a Denver Nuggets game and wouldn't be back until late. Strike two.

With only one swing left we headed east. On Vassar Street we stopped in front of a two-story blood-red brick home. The whole neighborhood was made of brick, the building material of choice in those days. In the yard stood Terence with basketball in hand, his frame several inches taller than Dennis, and heavier. He wore newer looking Reebok high-tops, black sweats with matching sweatshirt, and a Colorado Rockies baseball cap. The young African-American appeared to be in excellent shape, and extremely athletic.

Dennis explained to me he was a two-sport athlete—football and basketball the main focuses of his life. He dreamed of being an outside linebacker or power forward.

We left the car and Dennis greeted Terence happily. The two appeared to be close friends. I figured I wouldn't be pushy this time. The lad was built to blindside me. It had been a while since I'd woken up without any recollection of my name, and getting my butt kicked by a teenager might damage my tough guy image.

"This is Jarvis Mann," introduced Dennis.

"Good to meet you, sir," said Terence politely.

I shook the hand and found it strong and firm, the voice deeply baritone. He was damn close to my size but thicker and likely stronger, yet only a year older than Dennis. He had big wide brown eyes, short growth under his chin, and a noticeable scar running along the right side of his nose.

"Going to shoot hoops?" asked Dennis of his friend.

"Thinking about it. Got an hour of sun left. Care to join me?"

"I can't. Tomorrow I should have time after school."

"I'm sure you're here for something. Came to see my sister, I bet." He gave a sly glance to his friend.

"No, not today." Dennis seemed embarrassed. "I wondered if you've seen my Ernie Banks card. It's gone."

Terrance showed no reaction to the question.

"No man, I haven't. When did it go missing?"

"Somewhere between the time I showed it to you guys and when I got home. My father is going to be pissed." Dennis said morosely.

Terence nodded. "I can relate. I remember when I lost Dad's camera a couple of years back. I couldn't sit down for a week."

"If you see it will you let me know? It's worth a whole lot of money. Mister Mann is a private detective I've hired to help me find it."

"That sounds like an interesting occupation," asserted Terence. "It must be exciting chasing down the bad guys."

"Sometimes, but lately..." I stated while shrugging.

"Well, got to go before I lose all my daylight. A pleasure meeting you, Mister Mann. I'll see you at school tomorrow, Dennis, and we can shoot hoops afterwards."

Terence climbed onto his shining black eighteen-speed bicycle and pedaled off with basketball in hand.

"Strike three," I announced.

"What?" wondered Dennis.

"Just counting out loud. A baseball analogy since we're searching for a baseball card. I believe we've struck out. Anyone else you can think of who might have had access to it?"

Dennis gave it a few minutes thought. Thinking the worst of people didn't seem easy for him. Zero was all he came up with.

"How about someone in your family, maybe a sibling? A brother?"

"Yea, but I don't *think* he'd do it. He respects my stuff. Never had a problem with him taking anything of mine."

"Gee, I wish I could say that about my brother," I uttered. "He couldn't keep his hands off anything of mine. I'd always get in fights with him for using my bike and baseball mitt."

"I guess you didn't like him much."

"On the contrary. Though two years older, he saved my butt on a couple of occasions when someone was picking on me. Even if annoying, he went to the wall for me when necessary."

"I saved my brother a couple of times. When it's family..."

The time had come for me to use my years of experience. When faced with a problem I found it best to talk over your options with your client and a course of action may come to light you hadn't thought of.

"We need to think like the bad guy, Dennis."

Dennis nodded.

"Put yourself in their shoes. If you stole a valuable bubble gum card, or even found one, what would you do?"

"I'd try to sell it," he said without hesitation.

82

"Sell it where?"

"Someplace that buys collector cards."

"And is there one in the area?"

"There's one right on Broadway—Bill's Sports Collectibles. I've been inside many times."

"Good job," I declared. "You'd make a good detective. Let's take a trip to see if anyone has brought in an Ernie Banks rookie card to sell recently."

Dennis beamed at my praise as we got into the Mustang. The drive wasn't far, only a few blocks away and we arrived in short order. Since it was getting late on this Sunday, I hoped they remained open.

"If I was the culprit, I'd do one of two things," I expressed on the way over. "I'd either hold onto the card for a while to see if anyone missed it, or if in desperate need of money, I'd try to cash it in right away. My professional instinct says Bill's Sports Collectibles is the spot where we'll learn something."

Dennis agreed with me, though he didn't appear overly impressed with my deduction, since he'd already come to that conclusion on his own. It would seem few people ever were amazed with my skills. A reaction I'd gotten used to.

We found an open parking spot as Bill's seemed to be busy on this Sunday with four cars parked out front. The entire structure was theirs, the combination tan brick and green aluminum trimmed facing looking freshly remodeled. White security bars graced their windows, as well as sports posters depicting many of the greatest athletes. Their yellow sign showed the business name; the hours on the main door showed they'd be closing soon. We needed to be quick.

Inside, the whole store had wall to wall collectibles; programs, guides, books, autographs, jerseys, pins, pennants, caps, jackets, posters, and collecting accessories. They specialized in baseball and football cards but carried basketball and hockey as well. Glass cases displayed the various cards of thousands of athletes from all the different eras going back beyond my birth date. From every team you could imagine, and from teams which no longer existed. The prices for a small piece of cardboard were outrageous. And the wheeling and dealing led one to believe that sports cards were traded much like stocks on Wall Street. The common man's hedge against inflation—an investment in the future.

One could see the change on Dennis' face as he walked up and down the various cases, fixating in awe. It wasn't his first time here but that didn't matter. Displayed before him were his heroes staring back in two dimensions. It may be as close as he'd ever come to these athletes.

A salesperson greeted us, and I asked for the manager who thankfully was working. A few minutes later we were talking. His answers to my well thought up questions might clear up the mystery.

"We're looking for an Ernie Banks rookie card," I stated, getting right to the point.

"You're in luck," replied the manager. "We happened to encounter one recently."

I glanced at Dennis and could tell he knew we'd hit pay dirt.

"What condition is it in?" I asked.

"Nearly perfect. Stored in a penny sleeve and a top loader to protect it. The previous owner had taken wonderful care of it."

"May we see it?"

He led us to the rear of the store where he removed the card from the display case, so we could view it. The sticker with the name and address had been removed from the back, though the tacky residue remained. On the front, a new price tag listing a figure close to the book value. This certainly was the card.

"Can you tell me where you got this?" I inquired.

"We purchased the card yesterday."

"Can you give us a name?"

"That's privileged information I can't divulge. Why do you ask?"

I pulled out my ID. The picture was driver's license quality, making it lousy. It took him a minute to match the photo to the face.

"What's this about?" wondered the manager.

"Dennis here had his Topps Ernie Banks card stolen yesterday," I said while putting my hand on his shoulder. "It appears someone has sold it to you. He had his name and address labeled on the back, which has been removed. If you check you can tell it was once there."

The manager took the card in hand and felt the stickiness. He glared at me and Dennis for a moment, seeming to weigh the situation. He placed the card back into the display case and locked it.

"There is nothing I can do," he stated. "I'm sorry Dennis here has lost a valuable card. You've no proof he is the owner. His insurance will cover the monetary loss."

"We understand, and we accept the fact you're not to blame," I affirmed. "You made a straight business deal. But you can tell us who sold it to you."

The manager paused to contemplate. "I don't know."

"Please. This means more to me than the money." Dennis sounded extremely sincere. Please had worked wonders on me earlier. *Would it work now?*

The manager's eyes went back and forth between us, deciding what to do.

"I shouldn't do this. I don't know his name. He insisted on being paid in cash. Luckily, I had eight hundred dollars in the store. It is dangerous to keep lots of cash on hand these days." He stopped to reflect. "He was a little older than Dennis here, and bigger. He was black and appeared to be an athlete. He had one of those strange haircuts, short on the sides and longer on top, plus a little growth under his chin. What else? Oh, that's right. Now I remember. I noticed a scar on his face, along his nose. I asked him about it, but he didn't answer me."

"Terence!" came out of Dennis's mouth bitterly a second before mine, a flush of anger pervading his face. The culprit had been found.

"Thank you for the information," I said. "Much appreciated."

"If he confesses to stealing the card," stated the Manager, "I'll sell it back for what I bought it for. But hurry as it may not last long. I have it priced to sell."

"Sounds fair. We'll contact you."

Dennis and I walked out of the store. Anger seemed to well up inside, an emotion I couldn't blame him for having. If a close friend had ever done that to me, I'd have been furious too. Now the question was what to do.

"We go confront him," stated Dennis without hesitation. "He said he'd be playing basketball at the church."

It's what I'd have done. Though how will the lad react? Terence

85

was much larger, and probably stronger. But one did not steal from friends. I'd stand in the background and watch, for it was all I cared to do. It was between them to settle their differences.

In silence I drove until we pulled down the alley behind the church. A couple of basketball hoops lined the outer ring of the pavement in the middle of the lot. There, shooting in the fading light, stood Terence. As I watched, he expertly made every shot from fifteen feet away and at least for today, he was deadly accurate. The young man had skills.

Dennis didn't hesitate for a second. As soon as the car stopped, he was out the door and determined to extract answers. Following I stayed well back. I'd only interfere if the confrontation got ugly. The first words spoken were direct and to the point.

"I *know* you did it. I just can't figure out why." Dennis shouted with a touch of spitefulness, his right index finger pointed.

Terence seemed startled. He did not immediately respond.

"I see you've brought your stupid look with you. Little doubt from someone with half a brain lacking smarts. Did you think you'd get away with it?"

Terence took a shot and missed for the first time since we'd arrived. Dennis snatched the rebound and tossed the ball into the grass yard which got his friend's attention.

"Hey bro!! What the hell is up with you?" Terence had a confounded look.

"Don't give me your bull! You *know* what is up. You stole from me. A brother no less. How could you do that to me?"

Dennis now sounded like someone from the street. More so than at any time this day. I wondered what had brought it out. Was it the anger or the feeling of betrayal? You did not betray a friend.

His eyes now averted, Terence realized he was caught. He attempted to play dumb, though I figured him to be quite intelligent.

"The trading card! My Ernie Banks rookie card! You swapped it for money. Sold me out for the long green. Did you need it so bad that you stole from me? Give me a reason or I'll take you down!"

There was no fear in Terence, though confrontation wasn't on his mind. He tried to turn and walk away but Dennis wouldn't let him. He grabbed him by the arm and rose up on his toes, standing eyeball to eyeball. Terence attempted to pull away and the scuffle began.

This was less a fight than a wrestling match. Both rolled to the ground struggling to deliver a punch. Dennis landed a couple to the chest and shoulder, while Terence covered up and tried to push his smaller opponent away.

After a couple of minutes, I deduced little was being accomplished. I intervened by grabbing Dennis and pulling him to his feet. He wasn't happy with me, but I figured he'd gotten his best shots in. Sooner or later the larger Terence would put him down.

"Let me go," Dennis yelled. "I want to punch his lights out."

"Cool it!" I said firmly. It was the closest I came to the language of the streets.

"Ok!" Dennis calmed down some. He understood the moment was over. Nothing in the way of violence would happen right now. Still he needed to have an answer.

"Terence, I believe your friend here is hurt," I said with my 'Father Knows Best' tone. "He doesn't understand. All he wants to know is why, and I believe you're man enough to tell us that much."

Terence brushed off the dirt from his sweats and wiped the perspiration from his face as he got up. It was always hard to admit a failing. Somehow, I sensed there was more than simple greed to this lad's dirty deed.

"I'm sorry," he said morosely. "I had no choice. I didn't plan it, but I had to do something."

"Go on," I said while Dennis stood silently.

Terence couldn't look at either of us, his hands resting on his hips. "I found the card in the play yard over there. It must have fallen out of your pocket sometime while we were horsing around. I picked it up fully expecting to give it back to you. But then I remembered what you said when you showed it to us—how much money it was worth." He sighed before continuing. "I needed the greenbacks."

I thought the worst. Drugs, booze, gambling, or a payoff for gang related problems that plague our city. All those thoughts flooded my mind, and I felt guilty rushing to judgment before hearing the facts.

"Dad has been out of work for months," uttered Terence, his eyes now fixed on his friend's face. "He worked for twelve years with a company that recently went out of business. It came as a complete surprise to him. One day he was working—the next unemployed. He's been searching real hard, but can't seem to come up with anything. I can tell he's worried."

It was a sign of the times. The economy was weak right now. Bankruptcy and foreclosures were up, welfare and unemployment lines were long. Good honest hard-working people were having a rough go of it.

"His unemployment checks aren't large enough. He could pay the rent, the utilities, the car payment, or buy food. Sometimes he can cover two or three, just not all four. Mom's job helps, but it's not always full-time. They've juggled the money for several months now, even receiving help from family, but it's caught up with them. The deadline was nearing."

"What are you trying to say?" asked Dennis, his anger subsiding, his face filled with concern.

"We needed fifteen hundred dollars by the end of the month or we'd be evicted. Dad and Mom had scraped a little more than eight hundred dollars, but they realized it wouldn't be enough. They told us their problems, preparing us for the worst." Terence paused, a tinge of emotion in his voice. "I will live with Mom's parents, while my two sisters go to Dad's brother, while Mom and Dad move in with Grandpa and Grandma Williams. Mom wasn't happy with splitting the family up. It was tearing her up inside. And Dad, well we knew he was hurting for not being responsible for providing for us. You could tell he wanted to say he was sorry, but he couldn't. That wasn't his style."

"I gather you sold the card and gave your parents the money." It was the logical next question for me to ask.

"I agonized over it for a few hours," said Terence, his arms now crossed, his head hanging in shame. "It's not easy stealing from a friend right in the front yard of God. But given the circumstances, I had to do something. I felt helpless. Knowing my parents would be suspicious of where the money came from, I went to Bill's and got all the cash I could get, sealed it in an envelope and put it under the door with the word *gift* written on it. That way they'd figure it was an anonymous donor, someone from the neighborhood who'd heard of our troubles, or charity from the church. They had to take it then, and it was enough to get us by, at least for a while. I hoped things would look up for us now and give Dad time to find work again. He thinks he's got a good shot at a part-time position. The interview is tomorrow."

"Stealing isn't the answer," I asserted gently, hoping to make him understand. "There are better ways, and I'm sure you've come to that realization, because it currently shows on your face. The internal guilt will torture you until you come clean."

It was my best sermon in many a day. The one I'd given to myself numerous times when money had gotten tight and notions of crossing the line had creeped into my thoughts.

"Did your parents use the money?" asked Dennis softly.

"Yes, they did. They told us tonight the plans to move had been postponed for now. But they stressed to us the trouble was far from over."

Dennis stared for a long time at his friend. The anger and even the twinge of hatred had gone away. The sorrow for the misfortune of what Terence and his family were going through showed in his eyes. There would be no pity, at least not out loud. He stepped forward, extending his hand, Terence doing the same, the grip between them held for several minutes. Nothing more needed to be said.

After retrieving the basketball, we loaded his bike into my trunk, strapping the lid down with a bungee, and drove Terence home in silence. He got out and Dennis walked him to the front door, talking for a time out of earshot. I couldn't hear them and didn't want to. What they shared was most certainly personal. A moment between friends—among brothers, they would remember forever. A swirling orange glow filled the ebbing skies.

Dennis got back into the car and told me the money was no longer important. Terence could have it all to save his family. This was a gesture born out of deep feelings. In challenging times, we must make sacrifices. And a little piece of cardboard appeared small on the grand scale of things.

"What are you going to tell your father?" I asked as we pulled up in front of his house.

"The truth." Dennis seemed resolved of the proper action. "If he doesn't understand, I'll make him understand."

"I'll stand with you." This was my gesture of friendship.

"Thanks, but I'll do it myself. You must come inside. I owe you payment for the help you provided."

Getting paid seemed small after what I witnessed.

"I'm not sure I did much."

"You helped me to confront my problem. Not to mention drive me all over the place to find the card, making me realize material goods aren't the end all. You've earned your choice of one card from my collection."

I couldn't argue as the strength bled from the lad's broadening shoulders. I followed him into the house, where I stood in the foyer and waited.

Dennis returned with a thick leather-bound notebook of several hundred neatly displayed baseball cards in two-layer sleeves. We sat on the comfortable ebony sofa in the living room as I searched through each page carefully.

Most teams were represented, with cards from Hank Aaron to Todd Zeile, a catcher whose career started with my favorite team growing up, the St. Louis Cardinals. Players from the Chicago Cubs past and present were strongly prevalent. Though he had been traded to the Yankees the previous year, Alfonso Soriano was his current favorite player, his picture mixed in with other great Cubs. All the cards were in excellent shape. Many had value, others probably not much at all. Three of the collectibles stood out.

The first was a Mickey Mantle card, a Topps from the year 1964. It was the last time the Yankees had made the World Series for many years, and his last superb season before injuries brought a premature end to his career in 1968. With a good set of knees, there was little doubt he would have hit over 700 homeruns.

Then the greatest right-handed pitcher baseball would ever know. Sandy Koufax was the best left hander, but Bob Gibson was the most intimidating pitcher to ever play. This Topps 1970 card showed all his career stats, including the most dominating season a pitcher ever had in 1968. His 1.12 earned run average that year will probably never be matched and forced major league baseball to change the rules by lowering the pitcher's mound to add more offense to the diamond.

Finally, there was the Topps MVP card from 1961 featuring my father's favorite player of all time, and probably the greatest to ever play the game. Willie Mays had the grace and style tremendous athletes had. He could run, field, hit for power and average. His over the head catch in the 1954 World Series is legendary. Truly he was a marvel to watch. Though I'd only seen him play via archive footage, what he did was incredible and my father's stories of watching him play were etched in my mind. This was the card I wanted.

"Do you know the value of this one?" I asked, pointing to it.

"Not a whole lot. I believe twenty-five or thirty dollars at the most." Dennis seemed somewhat surprised. "I have a Henry Aaron card in there worth close to a hundred dollars. This would be more in line with our deal."

"Well Hammerin' Hank the homerun king was one of the greats. But Willie Mays was special to me. My dad told me stories of seeing him play in San Francisco when he was a kid. He did it all. Those were the tales which bonded us and what I remember best." I shook my head in happiness. "This card here is the one I want. Deal?"

Dennis wasn't about to argue. "All yours, Mister Mann."

"I think we've been through enough for you to call me Jarvis."

We shook hands in a more conventional way. I hadn't learned those complicated series of clasps yet. I hoped someday he would teach me.

"Hello," sounded a deep voice from outside the room. In walked a tall, strong looking man, a cautious smile working over his face. I stood to shake his hand and introduce myself. I left out my title for I didn't want to alarm him. The mere mention of private detective can make even the strongest men quiver. Dennis would explain to him later.

"Well, I'm sorry but I must to be leaving," I said. "I hope I can stop over sometime and take a closer view of your collection. It's quite impressive."

"I'd like that." replied Dennis rising from the sofa.

"Don't bother. I'll find my way out. A pleasure to meet you, Mister Gash." I shook his hand again and headed towards the exit. When I opened it, I heard Dennis speak to his father. "We need to talk, Pop."

I closed the door knowing what was coming. I figured he'd have no trouble making his dad understand and would take pride in how his son handled the situation. It was the kind of thing a generous man would do. He'd certainly matured today, as had I.

Driving home I knew right where I'd put the Willie Mays card, placing it in lower left-hand corner of the autumn mountain picture which hung behind my desk. When things looked down, and times had gotten tough, and the entire world seemed cruel and unkind, I'd stare at the card and remember a young man who'd learned to give and forgive, while facing responsibility all in the same day. With such heart, the future held hope if others like him emerged from this grim, greedy, selfish world. Maybe the 'me generation' would turn into the 'we generation'.

The thought of it all brought a smile to this cynical brow of mine. I stared into the rear-view mirror, for I'd forgotten what happiness looked like on my face. I enjoyed what I saw and wished to see it more often. One could only hope.

Thanks for reading *The Case of the Invisible Souls and The Case of the Missing Bubble Gum Card*. I hope you enjoyed both stories and would greatly appreciate if you would leave a review on Amazon to help an Indie Author. It is the greatest gift you can give us!!

I enjoy hearing from readers of my stories. Please email me at: rweir720@gmail.com

And be sure to go to my website for all the information about me and my books. You can also sign-up for my newsletter and I will send you a free eBook of the first novel, Tracking A Shadow.

https://rweir.net

If you love private eye mysteries, check out the rest of the Jarvis Mann Detective series and follow the evolution of my hard-boiled detective. I hope you enjoy all his adventures!

Tracking A Shadow, where Jarvis Mann is hired to track down the stalker of his sultry female client and is pulled into a web of lies and deceit.

http://www.amazon.com/dp/B00MQHVKJA

Twice As Fatal, where Jarvis works two cases that draw him into a seedy underworld, complicating his professional and personal life.

http://www.amazon.com/dp/B00XTNTHWW

Blood Brothers, where Jarvis is summoned back to his hometown of Des Moines, Iowa, to help his brother out of a life-threatening situation.

http://www.amazon.com/dp/B019S6AQXW

Dead Man Code, as Jarvis digs into a murder case of a computer software engineer and is confronted by Russian Mobsters and Chinese government goons, as all try to stop him from uncovering a crooked tech company.

https://www.amazon.com/dp/B01LY8JZND

The Front Range Butcher, Jarvis Mann faces a serial killer in a psychological battle of wills. Can he outwit such a mastermind, or has he met his match!

https://www.amazon.com/dp/B079MDS1K9

Mann in the Crossfire. Jarvis gets caught in the crossfire with deadly results.

https://www.amazon.com/dp/B07NDRWWSG

Follow R Weir and Jarvis Mann on these social sites as I appreciate hearing from those who've read my books:

https://www.facebook.com/randy.weir.524

https://www.facebook.com/JarvisMannPI

https://twitter.com/RWeir720

Made in the USA
Middletown, DE
13 July 2019